MASTERED BY

Doms of Destiny, Colorado 3

Chloe Lang

MENAGE EVERLASTING

Siren Publishing, Inc.
www.SirenPublishing.com

A SIREN PUBLISHING BOOK
IMPRINT: Ménage Everlasting

MASTERED BY MAVERICKS
Copyright © 2013 by Chloe Lang

ISBN: 978-1-62740-391-7

First Printing: August 2013

Cover design by Les Byerley
All art and logo copyright © 2013 by Siren Publishing, Inc.

Printed in the U.S.A.

PUBLISHER
Siren Publishing, Inc.
www.SirenPublishing.com

DEDICATION

This one is for Sophie Oak, Liz Berry, Chloe Vale, Shayla Black, Lexi Blake, and Lanae LeMore for all the love and support each of you continually give me.

I truly love you, ladies.

We're overdue for our three-margarita lunch.

How about we try for Friday at our favorite spot?

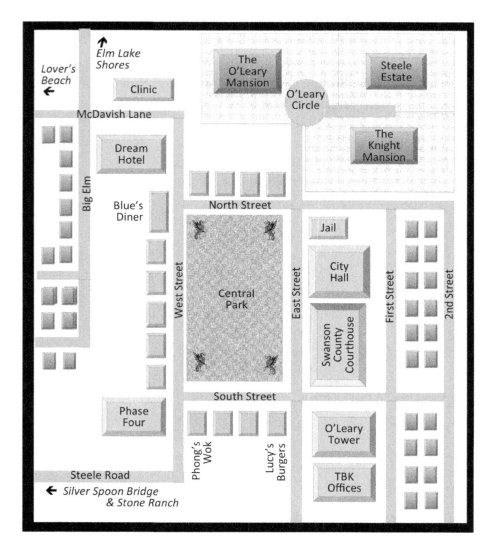

MASTERED BY MAVERICKS

Doms of Destiny, Colorado 3

CHLOE LANG
Copyright © 2013

Chapter One

Gut tightening and fingers shaking, Nicole Flowers held the phone to her ear.

"Hello, this is Sheriff Jason Wolfe." The man's voice was deep and authoritative, but she didn't give a damn how he sounded.

"And this is Officer Flowers of Chicago, Sheriff," she snapped. "Apparently you already know me, but I don't know you."

There was a pause on the other end and then an, "Ah."

"I just left my commander's office. I'm on suspension indefinitely because of you." Trouble always did like knocking on her door. "Why do you have it in for me?"

"Do you remember filing the missing persons report on Katherine White, officer?" the sheriff of Destiny, Colorado, asked.

"I do." It had been almost three months since she'd filed the report. Why was it coming up now? She chose her words carefully, knowing well how they could be twisted against her.

According to her mustached, asshole boss, her suspension began immediately. She should be clearing out her desk and heading for her apartment right now, but not before she looked through the database for the file Wolfe had used against her.

Hearing the sheriff on the other end brought the memory of her downfall to the forefront of her thoughts. Had it only been twenty-four months? Yes, though it felt more like several dark decades. In two days, it would be exactly two years to the date since the disaster. Another twelve days after that and her four-year service anniversary would arrive.

Two good years. Two bad years. Quite the resume.

Ancient melancholy oozed through every fiber of her being. Her past debacle was always cued up in her head for replay. An odd glance, a partially heard comment, or a pending peer review and the projector would fire up and play the movie in her mind again and again.

"Flowers? You still there?"

"Yes, Sheriff," she said, softening her tone. "Give me a second to pull this up."

The sheriff wasn't going to let go of this, and even though that had led to her suspension, she had to appreciate his ethics. That could mean trouble for her, which she definitely didn't need especially given her current status in the station. Quite a change from the legacy she'd inherited.

Her great-great-grandfather, Horatio Flowers, was one of the first Chicago police officers killed in the line of duty in the late 1800s. His youngest son Jeremiah Flowers, who had been only one at the time of Horatio's death, had joined the force years later. Jeremiah had three sons, one of them being Nicole's grandfather. All three became police officers with Chicago PD. Each, in their own way, had added to the family's legacy, but her grandfather had lifted the Flowers name even more, earning a slew of department citations, medals, and ribbons, including the Carter Harrison/Lambert Tree Medal for his act of bravery in a 1980s shootout between rival gangs in Cabrini-Green.

Skipping a generation, Nicole had been the pride of her granddad when she'd put on her badge. Thankfully, he'd died without ever knowing the black mark she'd put on her family's name because of one particular chain of events she couldn't seem to escape.

"Did you take the information down or did someone else?" Wolfe's question pulled her back from her thoughts. His voice was professional, but there was obvious aggravation in his terse tone.

The truth was it was Jaris who had given her the report to log into the system. Jaris—her former partner. God, she missed having a beat almost as much as she hated sitting at this desk. Everyone at the precinct loved Jaris—the polar opposite of how they felt about her. Jaris was the only person besides Patti who treated her with any semblance of kindness. If it weren't for him, she would've likely lost her badge completely.

"The investigating officer's name should be in the report, Sheriff."

"It isn't. Just your name."

That's odd.

To free her hand, she tilted her head so that the phone's receiver could stay in place between the side of her face and her shoulder. She typed on the keyboard to bring up an image of the report on her computer monitor.

The digital copy of the paper record filled her screen. Under her breath she cursed, seeing the investigating officer's field was empty. The only name from the station listed on the page was Nicole's as the police clerk. She'd scanned it into the system. She was a desk cop now. That was her job. How many reports had she filed in the last two years? Thousands? Tens of thousands? She should've noticed the error and brought it back to Jaris to correct, but she hadn't.

This is totally my fault, just like always. I should have checked. That's my job. As per normal, she felt like a total idiot. Her mistake had led to her suspension. But her commander had made it clear that it was much more than a clerical error that had put her in this awful situation.

"Officer Flowers, please enlighten me on why this report shows Katherine White as married to a man named Sergei, which is false. Ms. White is single."

Damn. This wasn't what she needed. The commander had to love this. He'd been looking over her shoulder for any bungle that he could use against her. This mistake had gotten her suspended. If anything else was uncovered during the investigation, it might end in her being off the force for good.

What then?

She was a cop. That was all she knew. It was all she had left after everything. It was the only thing that defined her. It made life bearable, if only slightly.

Sergei? The name sounded so familiar. Why? "Are you certain the woman isn't married?"

"Very certain, officer," Wolfe declared.

"It might be a typo, Sheriff. That does happen."

"Pretty big typo for Chicago PD, don't you think? A typo that ended in a body count of seven in my town. What do you think about that, Flowers? Sergei's last name wasn't White, and he wasn't married to Kathy."

Shit. This was bad. "Have you talked to the guy himself, Sheriff? He might have the answers you're looking for."

"He's one of the seven. Doubt if he has anything to say."

"His last name was?" She held her breath while she waited for the answer.

"Mitrofanov."

Slippery slopes seemed to find her no matter how hard Nicole tried to avoid them.

Sergei Mitrofanov. No wonder his first name had sounded so familiar to her.

The creep had been brought in for a drug possession charge six months ago. Of course, lots of creeps came through the station for the same kind of charge, but that one had been different for several reasons.

One, Sergei was the son of Niklaus Mitrofanov, a Russian mafia kingpin in South Chicago. Internal Affairs was presently on a witch hunt to flush out all the dirty cops in the department on Niklaus's payroll.

Two, less than twenty-four hours after his arrest, Sergei had been released because the evidence had been misplaced from the station, which resulted in a total mess for her and Henry Underwood, her grandfather's last partner and protégé. Henry had been a rookie back then, but later became her own mentor when she'd joined the force. They were both being scrutinized by Internal Affairs for the mishap. She was the station's administrator for all paperwork, which included cataloging incoming evidence. Henry had taken the job of managing the station's evidence locker six months ago to knock out the remainder of his time until retirement. Though he missed his beat, Henry's knees were shot. But Henry's golden years were on the line. They both needed to be cleared of any wrongdoing in the Sergei Mitrofanov case soon. If not, they might get suspended or worse— lose their badges.

Three, and the final thing that tied this horrible package up with a nasty little bow, the arresting officers that had brought in Sergei were Nicole's only two friends left in the station—Patricia Edmonds and Jaris Simmons. Patti and Jaris.

Navigating this mess might be more than Nicole could handle. Internal Affairs had already been a constant thorn in the district's side since Mitrofanov's release. Who could she talk to about what the sheriff was telling her? Normally, she would say Jaris, but now she wasn't so sure, especially given what she was reading in the report on the screen. It had come from him, a man she trusted. He'd pulled her out of some very hot water on more than one occasion. He had her back. Always. Didn't he still? She believed he did.

Should she talk to someone in IA about Wolfe's findings on the Katherine White missing person's case? She wasn't sure that would be a good idea since it was rumored that a few of them had been bought. Besides, would her word have any credence given her own record? No. It didn't matter anyway. Her commander probably was already on the horn with the higher-ups about this.

There was a contact number listed on the form.

"Hold on, Sheriff." She put him on hold and dialed the number.

It rang three times and then the voice mail picked up. "This is Sergei." The dead man's voice had the Russian accent she remembered from the day he'd been booked.

She clicked it off and looked around the station, which was quiet for a Friday night. She was about to punch the red flashing button to bring the sheriff back on the line when Patti and Jaris walked back in from their smoke break. Funny, since only Patti still smoked. Jaris had quit three years ago, but he had told Nicole he still loved the smell of a freshly lit cigarette.

Patti was tall for a female, nearly six feet, but looked small next to Jaris's six-five, muscular stature. Both were in uniform. He took off his hat, revealing his thick blond hair. Patti did the same, and her mane of dark locks fell to her shoulders.

Should I trust them? God knew she wanted to, but trust didn't come easy for her. IA thought there were dirty cops inside the station, and she was beginning to believe they might be right. With her suspension in play, she could finally take some of her built-up leave the commander had been pushing her to use. She'd refused, afraid of being away from the station, afraid of facing temptation, afraid of being alone. Was this the opportunity to do some real police work she'd been looking for?

"Sheriff, do you know where Kathy White is now?"

"Here in Destiny. Why?" he asked.

"Just getting all the facts straight." She needed to clear her name of this screwup. Talking to Ms. White might be a good start. The woman might know more about the Mitrofanov family than the sheriff believed. Why else would Sergei have somehow gotten his name on the report as White's husband? A few questions about any cross associates of the woman might eventually lead Nicole back to her station and the ties that the Russian had there.

If she succeeded, she might also be able to clear Henry's name, identify the officers who'd been on the receiving end of the Mitrofanov family, and give her own record a much needed boost.

But what if Jaris was at the center of the whole mess? Jaris was a friend. Better for her to find out before Internal Affairs did. She would give him the same favor he'd given her. It was the least she could do for Jaris.

When Patti waved at her, she punched the hold button.

"Are you there, Sheriff?" she asked.

"I am."

"I'll be in Destiny tomorrow."

Chapter Two

Nicole couldn't believe she was in danger, but Sheriff Jason Wolfe, his deputy, the former CIA agent, and the Russian guy had made quite the case that she might be.

"How do you know that?" she asked the dark-eyed man. "By your own words, you've been on several shit lists since leaving your old life. Who in the mob would still be talking to you?"

Alexei Markov shrugged. "Many peoples talk. I am friendly man. They also attempt to stab me, but luckily I am hard to kill." The enormous bear of a man leaned forward. "I would not to be steering you in misdirection."

And the big guy still seemed to be struggling with English.

Wearing sunglasses indoors, Dylan Strange, the former federal agent, turned to him. "When do you head back to Bliss?"

A brilliant smile came over the Russian's face. "Now. I am missing my heart's sweet. But do not to be worrying, I am working on idea to flush out badgers in Flower's station in Chicago."

"Badgers?"

Strange covered a grin. "I think he means moles."

"Badgers are better. You smoke badger from hole and badger tries to kill. Mole is just ugly. I do not understand why to call it mole." He sighed. "It's all right. I will teach you better ways."

"You have a plan?" she asked him. "What is it?"

"Not to be so impatient. We have old saying in Russia. Too many cooks in the kitchen makes for soup that blows up in face. These things to be taking time." The Russian stood and looked at Wolfe. "I will to be contacting when I am more sure. You understand?"

The sheriff nodded. "Make sure you do, Markov."

"Yes," Alexei said.

"I'll walk you out to your car." Dylan Strange stood from his chair and turned back to Wolfe. "Sheriff, if you need anything from me, give me a call."

Nicole watched as the big, might-be-just-the-slightest-bit-insane Russian and the former CIA agent left the sheriff's office. This wasn't what she'd been expecting to find when she'd decided to come to the tiny town of Destiny, Colorado.

Charlie Blake, Destiny's deputy, turned to her. "We have to make sure you are protected."

None of this made any sense to Nicole. "It's been three months since I filed that report. If I was in danger, why wait so long to contact me?"

The sheriff of Swanson County took a seat behind his desk. "I've been working with a man by the name of Nate Wright. He's the sheriff of Bliss County, Colorado. He's a former DEA agent, and since drugs are what brought Katherine White to Destiny in the first place, he's been using his old contacts to look into the case for me. He also introduced me to Alexei Markov. Alexei spent ten years working with the Russian mob before making a deal with the feds to testify against his old bosses. His testimony brought down one of Russia's biggest families and the people they were working with here in the States."

Nicole remembered it well. The trials had been headline news for months.

The sheriff took a sip from the coffee mug on his desk before continuing. "Markov encouraged me to hold off before contacting anyone in your department. He suspected the Mitrofanovs had officers on their payroll and he didn't want to tip them off. When he was sure your commanding officer was clean, I called him. Almost immediately, Markov's street contacts came back with word that Niklaus's men were looking for you. By that time you were already on the road here."

So Internal Affairs was right about the corruption in her precinct. How far up did it go? She couldn't just sit back and wait. She needed to start investigating, start asking questions.

"We can keep you safe while Markov works out his plan," Wolfe assured her. "I've got two men in mind for the job. Their place is very remote. They live off the grid. No one will be able to find you there."

She wasn't the type of person who sat back and waited while others took care of everything. Besides, she'd spent two years as a beat cop in Chicago. She knew how to take care of herself. "I don't need protection, Sheriff."

His eyebrows shot up. "Either you do as I say, Flowers, or I will be forced to call your commander. Does he know you came to Destiny right after being suspended? I bet he doesn't. He's looking for a reason to take your badge right now. Don't give it to him."

"Jason, calm down." Charlie ran a hand through his hair, obviously frustrated. "It's for your safety he's pushing this, Nicole," he added in a softer tone.

She'd come to Destiny to do real police work but now was being forced into protective custody of sorts. The sheriff was a serious by-the-book kind of guy. If she pushed him too hard, he would call her commander and a whole bunch of worms would come crawling out of the can, things she didn't want to deal with right now.

More than anything, she wanted to keep her job, her badge, her dignity—what was left of it. Her grandfather had told her that a good cop knew when to lay low and when to rush in. This was definitely a "lay low" time.

"Take me to your two men, Sheriff. I'll see what I think of them and then I'll let you know my decision."

"You've got a deal."

* * * *

Sawyer Coleman finished repairing the ceiling where some D-clamps had been pulled out by an overexuberant submissive at Phase Four, Destiny's world-renowned BDSM club. "All done."

"Thanks so much for this." Mr. Gold held the ladder. "With Sarge in New Mexico for the next two weeks, this room would've been closed until he got back if you hadn't fixed it. I can't have debris falling on members' heads. Not good, since it's booked solid by the Stones and their new woman, Amber."

"Glad to be of help for my bosses." Sawyer didn't really think of Emmett, Cody, and Bryant as employers, though on paper that was exactly what they were to him and his brother, Reed. They owned the Stone Ranch, and he and Reed kept it running—ranch hands in title but lovers of the land in reality. He was happy for the Stone brothers. The change in them was evident to everyone in town, including him. The rugged cowboys were completely in love with Amber.

The Stone brothers were more like family to him, as were Eric and Scott Knight. His and Reed's sister worked for the Knights at TBK, their billion-dollar company. Erica was the youngest and only female of the entire group of the original Destiny orphans. The plane crash that had taken all their parents had united them together in a strange way. Well, that and the O'Learys' kindness to all of them after the tragedy.

"Aren't you done yet?" Reed asked, walking into the VIP playroom. He held his Stetson in his hand. Thankfully, there weren't any subs around since it was still a few hours before the club went into full swing. Women seemed to love Reed's wavy blond hair as much as his blue eyes, and his brother didn't mind using that to his advantage whenever he could. Reed was two years his junior but just as good a Dom as he in every way. Reed was happy to wear the badge of "man-whore," which most in the club called him. "We've got to get back up the mountain right now or we're going to have to bunk with Erica in town again."

His brother's urgency was clearly false. Reed wasn't anxious to get back to work.

Sawyer shrugged. "Sis isn't going to put up with you or me another night. I'm done here." He took the first steps down the ladder, ready to get back to their cabin before nightfall.

"Damn. That means no playtime." Reed was a terrific brother and friend. They were in sync in so many ways. They loved the mountain more than town. They loved being in a saddle more than a truck. But Reed hadn't grown weary of the one-night stands like he had. Training subs was fun, but it didn't hold the appeal it once had. Perhaps that was the age difference. In December, Sawyer would turn thirty. Reed had another two years before he did.

"There is more than enough work for both of us back at the ranch. You and I both know it."

Reed shook his head. "Fine. Besides, we need to check on Connie."

"You bet we do."

The main herd was already settled into the ranch's biggest valley where there was plenty of grazing and a pond. They still had to keep tabs on them, even if they didn't have to run hay, because of the mountain lion they'd named Connie. Quite the hunter, she'd brought down a heifer last year, even though her meal of choice seemed to be mule deer by the skeletons he and Reed had found on the ranch.

"Hey, guys." Sheriff Jason Wolfe walked in.

Sawyer stepped off the ladder, focusing his attention on the woman following close behind Jason.

"Hello, miss." Reed moved around the sheriff and stood right in front of her. "I'm Reed Coleman," his brother said, extending his hand.

The raven-haired beauty didn't take it, which seemed to disappoint Reed by the frown that suddenly appeared on his face.

"Officer Nicole Flowers from Chicago PD."

A female cop? Damn, I wouldn't mind being arrested by her.

She wore jeans that revealed her curves perfectly. Her blue knit shirt clung to her full breasts, which would fit into his hands nicely. She topped the outfit off with a sexy jacket.

"My eyes are north of where you're looking, Mr. Coleman." Nicole didn't look amused.

Sawyer snapped his head up to her chocolate-colored eyes. She wasn't looking at him but at Reed. Apparently his brother had been taking in her physique just the same as he.

Nicole placed her hands on her hips instead of crossing them over her chest. The woman had moxie, that was for sure. He'd never cared much for moxie before, always going for the more subdued types, eyes down, trembling.

But clearly Sawyer's dick had different ideas now, especially when it came to Nicole's moxie. His cock jumped and his balls grew heavy.

His mind didn't seem to be in the driver's seat as much as his desire. Sawyer was sure Nicole's soft curves would feel wonderful in his grasp. Unfortunately, squeezing her as a "hello" wouldn't be the best introduction to Destiny. And by the demeanor he saw from her, it would likely be met with discontent and flailing arms and legs. God, even that picture sent hot pulses down between his legs, making his jeans even more uncomfortable.

"Do we need more law enforcement in Destiny, Jason?" Gold asked. "With Charlie moving to California next week to be with his kids, that leaves you short a deputy. Is Miss Flowers taking that position?"

"She's here temporarily," Jason answered.

Nicole turned her big brown eyes his direction. "I'm here to assist the sheriff with a certain matter."

She was the most beautiful creature he'd ever seen. Sure, other men might see her differently, believing the stick-figure models to be more attractive, but not him. Her attitude might be firm, but her shape was most definitely soft, calling to his fingers to touch.

"Introductions are in order," Jason said, always bent on the protocols both here at Phase Four and everywhere else. Rules. The law. That was Jason's way. "This is Mr. Gold. He owns the club."

This time, Nicole extended her hand. "Interesting place you have here."

Gold shook her hand. "Thank you. Are you familiar with my type of club, officer?"

"Like I said, I'm from Chicago," Nicole said. "Yes. I'm familiar."

"I'd be happy to extend you a visitor's pass during your stay in Destiny, officer." Gold smiled.

Sawyer leaned in, hoping she would accept the offer but knowing that was doubtful.

Nicole shook her head. "No thanks. I'm only here to help the sheriff. Nothing else."

Jason turned to Reed. "You've already met Reed Coleman."

"The pleasure is all mine, miss," Reed said, bending at the waist in a silly bow.

"I'm sure that's true, Coleman." The corners of Nicole's lips curved up slightly for a moment and then back down into a frown. Reed's devilish charm seemed to have worked on her if only for a split second.

God, he would love to see a full smile on her gorgeous face.

"And the guy by the ladder is…?" Nicole's brown eyes zeroed in on him, her long lashes fluttering.

"I'm Reed's brother, miss. Sawyer Coleman." He stepped forward, closing the distance between them, and put his hand out for her to take.

She smiled and took his hand in her tiny fingers. The connection felt electric, sending a hot current through his body and eventually settling in his cock.

"Nice to meet you, Sawyer Coleman. I'm sure you have your hands full with this one." She tilted her head toward Reed.

"More like the other way around," Reed said.

Nicole laughed. "I'm a police officer, Coleman. I know when

someone is lying to me, so don't even try it."

His brother's eyes narrowed. Nicole was getting to the man-whore like no woman had ever before. It was fun to watch. But she was also getting to him. Though their handshake had ended, he kept his fingers wrapped around hers, unwilling to let go of her for even a second.

"Don't be too hard on my brother, officer," he said. "He's not used to being around women like you."

"Like me?" she asked, pulling her hand free but keeping her gaze locked on him. "What does that mean?"

Sawyer immediately missed touching her fingers. "You're not blown away by his overused lines and floppy blond hair."

"Don't forget his big blue eyes. I bet the girls swoon over them." The amused grin on her full lips made his blood turn hot in his veins. "I like blue but I also like green, like yours."

Damn. He could already tell this girl was going to rock his world. "Nice to know, Nicole."

She blinked and her cheeks turned a gorgeous shade of red.

Sawyer's heart thudded in his chest like a jackhammer. She might have the body type he was always drawn to, but her manner, edgy and defensive, was calling to him, too, which was new. Why? What was it about this woman that had him reacting like a teenage boy and not a twenty-nine-year-old cowboy?

* * * *

Reed couldn't seem to keep his eyes off of the sexy Chicago police officer. He didn't understand his reaction to Nicole's arrival. Life had a certain flow that fit him quite well. Women were easy for him to read. He liked it that way. Liked it very much. He knew just how to flirt, to tease, to touch, to get what he wanted. And he always got what he wanted. Why was he having such a hard time getting into Nicole's head, and why was she so inside his? Getting into a woman's pants was as simple as *ABC*, but apparently she wasn't falling for that.

He thought with Nicole, he might have to go past *ABC* and all the way through the alphabet and back again, if that would even work. He wasn't sure. She might be a puzzle to him now, but he was determined to do whatever it took to solve this gorgeous mystery.

"Sawyer, you're as much of a player as your brother, aren't you?" Nicole's brashness floored him.

Damn it, what the hell is wrong with me? He'd never felt so unsettled about a woman in his life. He wanted her, wanted her more than anything. That was a problem, and he knew it. No matter how exciting and alluring she was, he needed to keep his head straight and his heart in check. *That is how I roll.* That was how he got through everything.

Sawyer sighed. "No one is as much a player as Reed."

She laughed, and everything inside him exploded with want.

More than desire or conquest, he could feel a new emotion growing inside him—the need to possess, to protect, to pleasure.

Nicole moved closer to him, and his temperature rose in his veins. "You two are trouble. I knew that the moment I walked in here."

God, he couldn't let himself imagine having the life his parents had. Their two dads were brothers, just like him and Sawyer. They'd found their mom on a trip to a livestock auction in Texas. A whirlwind romance later, and they were married and back in Destiny. Growing up in his parents' home had been so wonderful. They didn't have big bank accounts, but they had something worth so much more—love, real and enduring. At least until the plane crash.

The only way to get her out of my head is to get her into bed.

He grabbed her hands and held them up against his chest. "You have no idea what kind of trouble I can be, Chicago."

Chapter Three

Nicole tried to pull her hands free of Reed's hold but he wouldn't release them. "I may be in civilian clothes right now, cowboy, but I'm still packing." She was trying to remain calm and in charge on the outside even though her insides were quite the opposite. *Sheriff Wolfe wants these two to protect me from the Russians. Who is going to protect me from them?*

"That a threat, Chicago?" His blue eyes were the most piercing ones she'd ever seen, and they were undeniably slicing her into tiny, trembling bits.

"Does it need to be?" she asked, keeping her anxiety in check if only a little. Clearly, Reed and Sawyer were members of Gold's club, and she had a pretty good idea what that meant.

"Perhaps we're getting off on the wrong foot, darlin'." His deep voice rolled over her like a summer breeze, warming her skin. She detected a slight Southern accent from him, which only made him more intriguing to her.

"It's not my feet you're holding, Reed. It's my hands."

He smiled broadly, and her knees grew weak. "I like your hands, sweetheart. So soft and delicate."

"I'd like them back, if you don't mind," she said, hearing her voice come out harsher than she intended.

"I mind very much, but for now, I'll let you have your way." His big rough hands set her fingers free, but the tingling they'd ignited in them remained. "I'm fixin' to blow you away with some Colorado charm, Chicago. Prepare yourself."

The thought made her shiver. She had to get herself together. She was here to do a job, not to fall for a couple of handsome Colorado cowboys. Except he didn't really have the typical Western accent she'd heard before. "'Fixin' to'? Where did that come from?"

"My mother was from Texas. She imported it here." Reed's eyes turned from lusty to sad in a flash. Why? He spoke of his mother in the past tense. Did that mean she had died?

"Since the intros are done, let me get down to why I'm here with Nicole," Sheriff Wolfe said.

"Sheriff?" a voice called from the doorway.

Nicole turned to see a beautiful woman walk into the room. She wore her dark hair in a bun and had on a flattering gray suit. She held a briefcase by her side like a weapon.

The woman seemed hesitant. "Sorry to interrupt, but might I have a minute of your time?"

The sheriff turned around and faced the new arrival, clearly shaken by her. "Phoebe, what are you doing here?"

"Counselor, you're not here to serve me, are you?" Gold asked. "I know we've had our differences, but I can assure you all my records are in order."

An attorney. Nicole should have known when she saw the suit.

Phoebe looked to the club owner, clearly annoyed. "This isn't about you, Gold. If you don't mind, I need to speak with Sheriff Wolfe about a private matter."

Since meeting the young handsome sheriff, Nicole had found him to be demanding, self-assured, and unflappable. Something about this leggy lawyer clearly unhinged him. She wasn't sure what had happened between these two, but there obviously was history involved. Whatever passion they'd had in the past must have hit the skids a while back.

The sheriff's fists clenched in obvious frustration. "I'll be back after I find out what Miss Blue has to say. Nicole, please stay here with Reed and Sawyer. I've got more to discuss with the three of you."

She nodded, and the duo stepped out of the room through the same door she'd entered.

Gold folded up the stepladder and held it in his arms. "I'm going to put this up. I'll be in my office if any of you need me." The owner of the club walked to another door at the opposite side of the room, leaving her alone with Reed and Sawyer, the two beautiful cowboys who were ramping up her anxiety to the max.

Being alone with them was adding to the little quakes already inside her. What was wrong with her? *I'm a cop.* She wasn't one of those women who needed a man. Never had. Never would. She was self-reliant. Always. *Then why am I shivering?* The room wasn't cold.

"This might be a good time to get to know each other better." Reed looked her straight in the eyes, and she felt her whole body begin to melt. "Chicago, you have family in the Windy City?"

Her gut tightened as her constant companions, guilt and grief, wrapped their claws around her insides. "No. Just me."

Sawyer cupped her chin, causing her to catch her breath. "You're alone?"

God, he was so devastatingly handsome.

This was none of their business. "I have family, just not in Chicago anymore," she lied.

He sighed, removing his hand. "Not true. I know. Reed and I lost our parents a while back. I know loss when I see it, and I definitely see it in your face, Nicole."

She felt her eyes widen in shock. How could he see into her so easily? It was unsettling. She tightened her jaw, willing her internal walls to thicken. With her guard back up and in place, she wanted to get back to the case at hand. Even if Wolfe and Alexei were right about the Russians looking for her, how would they know she was in Destiny? The Coleman brothers definitely looked the part as big, brawny protectors, but she had her pistol. With it, she could handle just about any asshole who dared to show up.

While the sheriff remained in the hallway with Phoebe, Nicole thought it would be a good idea to interrogate these cowboys.

She'd start with the easy question. "Do either of you know Katherine White?"

"You mean Amber?" Reed nodded. "Yes."

"No, I mean Katherine White." She'd never heard of the other woman. "She was missing for a few days about three months ago. Who is Amber?"

"Same person," Sawyer interjected. "She had amnesia, so the Stone brothers, the guys who found her, started calling her Amber. After her memory returned, the new name suited her more. That's what everyone in town calls her now."

"Except her sister, Belle. She still calls her Katherine." Reed seemed to be studying her like she was a newly discovered species.

Though everything inside her pushed her to look away from his intense stare, she didn't. She needed to hold her ground or she would lose this battle of wills, and Reed's seemed to be limitless.

"What about Sergei Mitrofanov?" she asked, resisting the urge to chew on her lower lip like a silly schoolgirl. *What's wrong with me?* It wasn't like she was an innocent. She'd had sex, though not as much as most in the station thought. Unfortunately, most of her sexual experiences had occurred during her low time, which meant her memories of them were clouded. Guilt scraped the inside of her head, making her wince.

"I know he's dead," Sawyer interjected.

"Is that why you're here in Destiny, Chicago? Investigating the bastard's death?"

She'd said too much already. "I think I should be asking the questions here, not you two mavericks."

Sheriff Wolfe walked back into the room, but Phoebe wasn't with him. The look on his face seemed to indicate whatever she'd said to him wasn't good.

"Everything okay?" Sawyer asked.

The sheriff frowned. "The parole board approved Shane Blue's release. He'll be back in town soon."

"Damn…" Reed shook his head. "What happens now?"

"Miss Blue is concerned that I'll give her brother hell when he returns. I assured her that as long as he stays out of trouble, I'll leave him alone." The sheriff turned his attention to her. "I'll say the same to you, Flowers. I'll be the one asking the questions. This is my town. You're on suspension, not on duty. Remember that."

She had no idea who this Shane person was, but Sheriff Wolfe clearly wasn't happy to have him back in town. The harshness she'd heard during their phone call yesterday was back in full force.

"What do you need from us, Jason?" Sawyer asked. "Nicole mentioned something about the Russian who lied about being Amber's husband."

"She did?" The lawman glared at her. "What else did she say?"

She didn't like his demeaning tone and wasn't about to let it slide without a fight. "I'm not a rookie, Sheriff."

"Maybe not, but Chicago PD took you off your beat two years ago and chained you to a desk job, right?"

Had her commander shared all her black marks with Wolfe? If not him, then who? "I like working the desk."

Reed snorted. "Not true. I may not be law enforcement, Chicago, but even I can tell you're lying about that."

Sawyer stepped between her and the sheriff as if he meant to defend her from him. It only made her angry.

"Move out of my way, Mr. Coleman. I've been taking care of myself for a very long time. I don't need you to try to protect me, especially not from a fellow officer of the law." She held up two fingers. "I have been awarded two accommodations from my department. One was for sharpshooting and the other was for martial arts. Which would you like to see a sample of? Or will you trust me that I can handle whatever crap comes my way."

Sawyer turned to her, his face showing kind concern. "You've had more than your fair share of crap, Nicole, I'm sure. Too much, I bet."

His words softened her instantly, but she couldn't be vulnerable, no matter how much she wanted to be. Strong. She had to remain strong. She rolled her eyes, hoping the gesture would push him back some. It worked. He shook his head and stepped away, and she immediately regretted her success.

"I don't have time for this shit," the sheriff barked. "Flowers, you know you're in danger. Alexei's intel is spot on."

"Maybe so, but that doesn't mean the Mitrofanovs know where I am, Sherriff."

"I got a call from a guy named Henry Underwood. You know him?"

"Yes." Why had Henry called the sheriff? He was her last connection to her grandfather. He was the one person she still trusted. She'd called him on the road to Destiny and filled him in on what she was working on with Sheriff Wolfe. "I don't understand? Henry knew I was coming here. He's the only one I told. He didn't seem overly concerned at the time."

"Well, he is now. Henry has been working to clear your names, too, Nicole. Did you know that?"

"Figures. Henry's a good cop. He's not going to roll over without a fight."

Wolfe nodded. "Got to admire that in any officer." He continued, "Turns out that Alexei wasn't the only one to dig up info on the Mitrofanovs. Right after you left Chicago, Henry got a tip that the Russians were looking for you, too. That's when he called me to make sure you had protection in Destiny. Niklaus Mitrofanov has been released by the feds, you know."

Of course she knew. It had been all over the local news.

"Niklaus?" Reed's eyelids were narrowed.

"The Russian mobster who was the dad of Sergei. The prosecutors had to let him go since the two thugs we captured here in Destiny were killed in a car bombing during transport to a safe house." The sheriff's face darkened. "Fuck. Those creeps were ready to sing like canaries to get their sentences lessened. Now we're back to square one."

Worry pricked the back of her mind. "I'm still not sure why I'm on the Mitrofanov family's radar." *Is someone at the station trying to frame me? I'm not sure why. I'm no threat to anyone there.*

"Their mole inside your station must've found out you were looking into Amber's missing persons report. You're a loose end, and the Mitrofanov family doesn't like loose ends. They might also believe you have uncovered more about Sergei's drug possession arrest and it will eventually lead back to Niklaus." The sheriff let out a long breath. "Now that he's free, he's going to make sure he stays that way."

"That's why you want us, right?" Sawyer asked. "To be Nicole's bodyguards."

"I don't need bodyguards." she reiterated. "Let Niklaus's men come. I'll be ready."

Reed shook his head. "Not happening, Chicago. Not a chance."

She was a cop. They weren't going to treat her like some helpless female who needed a man to rescue her. "Who are you to tell me what to do, cowboy? We just met."

Reed put his big hand on her shoulder. "Maybe so, but trust me, you're not going to walk around Central Park like some kind of lone gunslinger ready to bring down the bad guys, accommodation in sharpshooting or not."

"Enough of this shit." The sheriff stepped right in front of her. "I've been in office for two years. You know how many murders Destiny had during the last sheriff's twenty years of service? Two. I've already had eight. I won't have your blood on my hands, Nicole."

She didn't need anyone to protect her. "You don't have a say in what I do or don't do, Sheriff."

A ruthless look crossed the sheriff's face. "Flowers, you're going to go to their cabin with them." Then the lines in Wolfe's face softened. "Go with them, Nicole. One police officer to another, would you do this for me?"

She'd heard that final phrase from her grandfather more that a few times. Jason reminded her of how her granddad saw the world. Black and white. She'd learned there was a whole lot of gray in it, too. "I want to, Jason, but I'm really here to clear my name. Can't you understand where I'm coming from?"

"Totally, if I were in your shoes. I promise to work on this with you, but I can't do the kind of job I need to if you aren't safe. I swear on my badge that these two are good guys. I would trust them with my own life. You can't risk any more problems. They'll be strong for you. That's why I chose them for you."

There was only one thing Wolfe could mean by that. He knew her secret. "Okay," she said, defeated. "Promise me you'll keep me in the loop on this investigation."

"I will. I swear."

She suddenly realized it hadn't been her commander who had shared her dark past with him. The one and only man still living that she still trusted—even though he likely thought it was for her own good—had betrayed her. "Henry told you all about me, didn't he?"

Sheriff Wolfe nodded.

The truth of her situation crushed her into a million bits of debris. *I'm alone in this.*

Chapter Four

"You okay, Nicole?" Sawyer edged Jason out of the way to take his place in front of her. Jason had hit some kind of button in her with his words and the color in her face had drained away.

She turned to him with eyes full of determination and fire. "I'm fine."

He knew better. She was obviously putting up a front to protect herself.

"What's it going to be, Officer Flowers?" Jason was not going to budge on this. It was clear that he wanted her guarded and out of the city limits for her own good.

He glared at the sheriff. "Back off, Jason. Give the woman some breathing room."

"Coleman, you and Reed weren't my only choice to see to her safety. Should I have picked Dylan and Cam instead?"

Jason was a friend, but right now the sheriff was pushing his limits. "Reed and I will take care of her."

"Nobody needs to take care of me." The hurt he'd seen in her face was gone, replaced now with a don't-you-dare-fuck-with-me look. Nicole was tough. Really tough.

"Gotcha," Jason said, pulling out his cell from his jacket. "I won't have your blood on my hands if the Russians show. Time to let your commander in on your whereabouts."

Sawyer could tell Jason was bluffing, evidently hoping to nudge Nicole into what he wanted from her—going with them up to their cabin. The idea suited Sawyer, too. The sexy policewoman would make great company. Very great company for sure.

Seeing her eyes widen in worry impacted him in a way he'd not felt before. He had the distinct urge to wrap her up in his arms and tell her everything was going to be okay. He wanted to protect her from whatever she was running from. He wanted to take the troubles she'd clearly been carrying for far too long and lift them off her shoulders.

"Chill, Jason," he said, hoping to quell Nicole's uneasiness. "How you won your election with your attitude is a mystery to me."

"I won fair and square," the sheriff barked. "You have no idea what kind of mess this woman is in."

"Fill us in," Reed said firmly. "Don't keep us in the dark."

"No need," the raven-haired beauty stated. "I'm going back to Chicago. This was a big mistake."

The thought of her leaving before he got a chance to know her stabbed him with a sudden jagged alarm. "Wait, Nicole. Jason's a lot of things but he isn't Destiny's best person to welcome visitors."

"And you are?" She shrugged away. "I came here to help with an investigation. If that's not what he wants"—she pointed at Jason—"so be it. I'm outta here."

Reed stepped in front of her, blocking her way to the door. "Stubborn, aren't you, Chicago."

"You have no idea how stubborn I can be, cowboy. Now, if you don't want your balls handed to you on a platter, I suggest you move aside."

"You can't go back until this mess is sorted out. It's too dangerous for you back in Chicago right now." Jason punched the buttons on his phone. "Let's see what your friend Henry has to say, Flowers. Maybe he can talk some sense into you."

"Stop." She rolled her eyes and then stared at the ceiling for several long ticks of the clock. When she returned her gaze back to them, the deep-seated hurt in her eyes flattened him. "You win, Sheriff, though I'm not sure why you are so set on pissing me off."

Jason put his cell away. "Not my intention. I just don't want the body count to go up in Swanson County. Let me handle this. I promise to keep you in the loop. Once I have a better handle of things, I'll bring you in."

Sawyer could tell the sheriff hated being an asshole to her, but like always, his friend did what was necessary to get the job done. Of course, Jason had lost Phoebe, the love of his and his brothers' lives, long ago because of his unbending ethics. Very sad.

"One week, Sheriff. That's all," she said. Jason had won the battle with her but not the war. God, what wasn't to like about this woman? "Do we have a deal or not?"

"Deal." Jason turned to Reed and him. "Take her to your cabin. I'll be up day after tomorrow with what I find."

Reed gave a mock salute. "My pleasure, Sheriff." As he turned to Nicole, Sawyer was surprised to see something new in his brother's face. He was more than a little intrigued by her. "Seriously, my pleasure."

"Our cabin is very rustic, Nicole." Being near her, inhaling her sweet musky floral scent was sending sparks through him and swelling his dick. God, she smelled good. "Perhaps we should ask the Stone brothers if we could use their house in town. They've been living in their cabin with Amber pretty much all the time since finding her."

"I'm not a princess. I'll make do."

"You're our guest. Naturally, we want you to be as comfortable as possible." He needed to be several steps ahead of her if they had any chance of spending more time together, which was what he wanted more than anything at the moment. "Why don't we take you to the cabin to see what you think about it. If you're okay with it, then we'll stay. If not, we can drive over to the Stones' cabin and get the keys to their house in town."

"Are you deaf, Sawyer?" Jason shook his head. "I told you that she needs to be kept out of town and out of sight. The Russian mafia isn't something to play around with."

Nicole sighed in obvious frustration. "You guys are too much. See this." She opened her jacket and revealed a Glock that was holstered underneath. "I'm not defenseless. Okay?"

A pistol-packing doll. Hot damn.

Reed smiled and walked to the table where they'd put their guns. He wrapped his belt with his holstered Ruger forty-five around his waist. "Neither are we." Reed grabbed up the other weapon, his Colt, and walked it over to Sawyer. He turned back to Nicole. "Should the commies come knocking, isn't it smarter to triple your odds, Chicago?"

"Seems I'm outvoted here in Podunk, Colorado." She put her hands on her hips.

The sarcasm wasn't lost on any of them, but Sawyer wasn't taking the bait. "Nicole, give us a chance."

"It seems I don't have a choice."

"You always have a choice with me," he told her honestly.

"What's it going to be?" Reed asked, his sudden fascination so evident it nearly filled the entire room.

She sighed. "I'm game. My car is parked outside the sheriff's office."

Sawyer shook his head. "I doubt it will make it up the mountain. What are you driving?"

"A Honda Civic. Why won't it?"

"The roads are mostly dirt and the majority of them take a four-wheel drive on good days to get up to our cabin. On bad days even more so."

"Fuck." The swear word on her pretty lips shouldn't have surprised him, her being a cop and all, but it did. "Fine. Let's go then. I need to get my stuff out of my car though."

She marched out the door, clearly in a hurry to get this over with.

"Damn, Jason." Reed blew out a big blast of air. "What have you gotten us into?"

"I guess you two will soon find out." Jason's shoulders sagged. "I know she's a cop, fellows, but with everything I've found out about her in the last couple of days, I know she's in real danger. She's got to be protected."

"We're on it, buddy." Sawyer rushed out of the room to Nicole, the woman who needed Reed and him. When he finally caught up to her, she was already walking past the Blue Dragon across from Lucy's.

She turned and rewarded him with a hint of a smile. "Your sheriff needs a course in manners."

"You've got that right."

"I think your brother isn't far behind him in that department either."

"Right again." As they continued down South Street, he watched her taking in the sights of his town. "Destiny has to be quite a change from Chicago."

"Yes, but take away the trees, mountains, and songbirds and add in throngs of people, high-rises, and screaming sirens and it's exactly the same. Have you lived here your whole life?"

"I have," Sawyer said as they turned onto East Street. "It's a great place to grow up."

"Any other siblings besides your brother?" she asked.

"Yes. We have a younger sister. Erica."

"I bet your parents had their hands full."

The old grief stirred inside him. God, he missed his parents. "This is our truck," he said as they passed Maude, the 1976 yellow four-by-four Chevy truck that had over two hundred thousand miles on her. They'd rebuilt her engine seven years ago. The old girl was once again on her last leg. The best course would be to junk Maude and buy a newer truck, but neither he, Reed, nor Erica could seem to let go of her. Maude had been their dads' last vehicle.

"This is mine," she said, pointing to the silver Honda next to Maude.

"Isn't that interesting that we are parked next to each other? Maybe this is fate playing out."

"I'm not a big believer in such things." She unlocked her door and pulled out a small suitcase. "Why didn't you park the truck in front of your club instead of a block and a half away?"

"Reed and I only come to town a couple of times a week. Today's trip started with a visit to the courthouse to get a copy of a deed to an acre of land we just paid off. Helping Mr. Gold, the owner of Phase Four, was the last task for today."

"It's early. What was your plan for the rest of the day?"

Reed walked up alone. Jason hadn't come with him. "Whatever we had planned, Chicago, is off. You're our one and only priority now."

She shoved her suitcase into his chest and smiled. "Good to know. Make yourself useful, cowboy, and put my bag in your truck."

Reed's eyebrows shot up and then a big smile spread across his face. "It's going to be fun being your bodyguard."

Nicole shook her head and shut her eyes. "One week. Only one week. I can handle this."

"And we can handle you, Chicago. You'll see."

"Reed, shut your mouth. Nicole is our guest. Stop teasing her."

"Sure thing, bro." Reed swung her suitcase into the bed of their truck. Then he opened the door. "Officer, if you please," he said in a mocking British accent.

She snorted but didn't say a word in response. She got into the truck, sliding past the steering wheel to the center of the cab.

Reed got in the driver's side of Maude and he took the passenger seat.

They headed out of town together.

The whole drive, she sat staring straight ahead with her hands on her knees. Touching her on the chin earlier had him hard as a rock, but this was no time to let his cock do his thinking for him. She needed him to be better than his best, and he silently vowed to himself that whatever it took to be that man, he would. No woman had moved him in that way before.

He wanted to hold her, to tell her everything was going to be okay, to kiss her until the hurt he sensed in her vanished for good. The load she carried was heavy. He could see it in her eyes, hear it in her words, even feel it around the false façade of toughness she presented. Of course, she was tough. Tougher than most men. She'd nearly had Jason on the ropes back at Phase Four. That was something to see.

He glanced over at her as Reed turned off the main road and through the cattle guard at the southern entrance to Stone Ranch. The firm set of her jaw told him a storm of doubt and confusion was brewing behind her big brown eyes.

Sawyer wanted to reach her somehow. This had to be difficult for her. It would be for any woman. She and Jason had told them about the error on the missing persons report and her suspension. She'd come to Destiny to clear her name. Now she was headed up a mountain with two strangers and the Russian mafia was coming for her. "Difficult" fell short of what she had to be feeling at the moment. He needed to lighten her mood. "Welcome to Stone Ranch, Nicole."

She turned to him for a brief moment and sighed. Then she turned back to staring straight ahead.

"It'll take us forty more minutes to get to our cabin." Reed turned the wheel, navigating around the debris in the road. "We're still cleaning up from a storm we had back in May. That was one helluva deluge. Most of the roads are back to normal. A few, like this one, still need work. Normally, the drive to our cabin would only take twenty minutes from here."

Reed knew what he was doing, and that made Sawyer proud of him. She wasn't a sub they needed to train, but she did need them. Keeping the conversation casual might help her to relax.

"Oh my God." Nicole's whole body seemed frozen with fear.

Her sudden outburst got his attention instantly, and his fingers unsnapped his gun's holster.

"What?"

She pointed straight ahead. "What's that?"

He looked in the middle of the road and saw the mountain lion he and Reed had learned to respect. Hell, they were even fond of the old girl. "That's Connie."

And then the big cat was gone.

"Odd for her to act that way," Reed said.

He agreed. They'd only seen her a handful of times in the last five years and then only briefly. "I think she came to welcome Nicole." He turned to Nicole only to find she was trembling. "Don't worry about Connie. This was unusual for her to be on the road. She avoids humans."

"She's so…so beautiful." Not only was Nicole sexy and beautiful and strong, but she was also obviously so, so passionate.

Sawyer had never met a woman like her before. A part of him stirred, but for the first time in his life, it wasn't his cock. It was his heart.

Chapter Five

The creature's gaze seemed to reach past all of Nicole's walls and into her soul.

She'd been so moved by the sight of the mountain lion. Connie was graceful and majestic. The big cat's size was impressive, at least seven feet, with her regal tail making up a third of her length. Connie's coat was a rich bronze. The tips of her ears and tail were black. Her memorable face was a grayish brown with a pale patch above each golden, mesmerizing eye.

"What can you tell me about Connie?" she asked, dying to know more.

Sawyer's big manly lips curled up into a sexy smile. "She's a loner."

Like me.

"And powerful," Reed added. "Connie's brought down some big game. Her favorite meal is mule deer, but she's also good at keeping the coyote population on the ranch to a minimum."

"She's actually snacked on some of the Stone's livestock. That's why we have to keep tabs on her. Connie usually hunts at night or during the low-light times of day, at dawn and dusk." Sawyer's voice was filled with what sounded to her like respect and reverence. "She's a mix of stealth and power. Last year I had the rare opportunity to see her through some binoculars patiently stalking a mule deer. She took her time, creeping up so slowly I could barely detect movement. She took the beast down in a single pounce."

Nicole closed her eyes, imagining how Connie had looked on that day. "Impressive. But I'm surprised you don't hate her. I thought most ranchers despised big cats and worked hard to eliminate them from their land."

Sawyer's hand came down on her knee, sending a tingle up and down her spine. She thought about asking him to remove it, but didn't. Of the two brothers, he seemed less forward than Reed. "If Connie keeps to mule deer and leaves the cattle and sheep alone, she can roam the Stone Ranch for as long as she likes. If her tastes change, then we will have to deal with her in a different way."

She knew that meant he and Reed would kill the beautiful creature. Like her, Connie was alone. "Does she hunt only on this ranch?"

"Nope. She's been spotted on the Knights' ranch as well as others. My guess is her range is wide, likely thirty-five square miles, but Stone Ranch is at the very center of it."

"Do you have Internet at your house?" she asked, hoping to read up on Connie's ilk. She wanted to see if mountain lions were on the endangered species list, if they ever attacked humans, and if so, how many fatalities occurred from big cats.

Reed drove the truck through another cattle guard. "No Internet or cell service, Chicago. We're way up the mountain. Very remote."

Her nerves went into high gear. She pulled out her cell and saw the infamous "No Service" message at the top right of its screen. "What about a landline? Surely you have a landline."

Reed shook his head. "It would've cost a butt-load to get the phone company to drop poles this far up. If you need to call someone, there's a payphone at the gas station we passed on the county road after we left town."

Sawyer squeezed her knee gently, startling her. She'd forgotten he was still touching her. "We don't have to go that far, Nicole. Most cells get a bar or two back near the entrance to the ranch. If you need to make a call, that's where we'll take you."

"Good to know." But she didn't have a single person she would call. Henry was number one on her speed dial, but she wasn't sure why anymore. He'd called Sheriff Jason Wolfe and told him her secrets, secrets that gave the sheriff the advantage over her. Why? Likely it was Henry's way of keeping her away and safe, but that didn't matter to her. He'd betrayed her. She wasn't sure she would be able to forgive him for that. She definitely wouldn't trust him again.

What about Patti or Jaris? They were number two and number three on her speed dial. No. She had to go through this alone, had to figure a way to get Jason to trust her to be on the case again, had to redeem herself of all her past sins.

"How much longer until we get to your place?" she asked.

Reed patted her thigh. "One minute to Castle Coleman. This is the entrance to our fifty-two acres."

"You have your own land?"

"Yep," the brothers said in unison.

Reed smiled, pride clear on his face. "Every year we try to buy an acre or two, depending on what we can save up."

"Isn't fifty-two acres enough to have your own ranch business?" She looked ahead and saw a wooden gate with a metal sign to its side. She smiled at the red-lettered message.

You are entering Coleman Territory. If friend, welcome. If foe, best to turn around now.

"No, Chicago. Here in the Colorado Rockies, you need a lot of land to run livestock, much more than what you need in flat pastures. On the Stone Ranch, you need about 10 acres for each head of cattle or two head of sheep."

"Water is the most important element, Nicole," Sawyer said. "There's our pond." He pointed to the left of the road at a pool of water that screamed for an artist to immortalize it in paint. The trees around it were magnificent. Its surface was like glass.

"We're here," Sawyer announced. "What do you think of our estate, sweetheart?"

The truck stopped and she gazed out the windshield to two structures. "Is that your home?" she asked, pointing to the bigger of the two buildings off to the left.

"Nope. That's one of our barns." Reed pointed to the small structure. "That's home."

She gazed at the tiny log cabin with a broad covered porch that seemed to wrap around the whole building. Two rocking chairs and a porch swing allowed visitors to take in the picturesque scenery around the wooden abode.

"Well?" Reed asked impatiently. "Do you love it or hate it?"

"I think it's the most beautiful place I've ever seen, but what difference does that make? I'm here because your sheriff forced me to go with you." Nicole saw the disappointment in Reed's face. She hated how easy it was for her to push people away. They'd been nothing but nice to her. They didn't deserve her rudeness. "It does look amazing though."

Reed smiled. "It's not much but it's all ours. We built it ourselves."

"You're kidding, right?" The cabin looked like it had been right where it sat for the past century, if not longer. Her first impression was that this was a home Mother Nature had built herself to live in. Nicole half expected the logs to sprout new growth right before her eyes.

"Reed and I aren't big kidders, Nicole. That would be our sister's specialty." Sawyer hopped out of the truck and held the door for her. Apparently, this part of the country still held to certain practices like men opening doors for women. She wondered what other past practices Destiny conducted on its streets.

"She live here, too?" she asked.

Sawyer shook his head, taking her hand and helping her out of the truck. "Nope. She lives in town."

She tensed, realizing she'd agreed to Sheriff Wolfe's demand to stay with Reed and Sawyer. One week here. The place looked tiny. "How many bedrooms does your house have?"

"You'll see." Holding her bag, Reed came around the front of the truck and stood beside her, which placed her right between him and Sawyer. Apparently, they were already assuming their bodyguard duties.

Her heart was pelting the inside of her chest hard and fast. She'd been in some tight spots back when she was still in the field with the department, but somehow this seemed scarier to her than any of those times.

"How long have you two lived here?" she asked.

"August it'll be ten years," Reed said with obvious pride. "Want to see inside?"

Her legs felt wobbly, but she still took a step forward. The brothers walked behind her as they moved onto the porch. She turned around and saw the mountain peaks off in the distance and imagined how amazing it must be to sit and enjoy the sights and sounds of nature. The sights and sounds of Chicago were much more chaotic and jarring.

She sighed, knowing she would be returning to the Windy City in a week. "I bet your sunsets are gorgeous here.

"They're nice, but it's the sunrises that take your breath away. We're facing east now, Chicago." Reed opened the door to the cabin. "I can't wait to see your face tomorrow morning at dawn."

"How early do you get up?" She'd never been much of a morning person, but imagined that both these guys were. "Don't tell me you're one of those people who leap out of bed with a smile."

"Sawyer's not but I am," Reed said, pointing to Sawyer.

Sawyer shook his head, clearly not understanding his brother's love of mornings. "Nicole, maybe you can explain to him why coffee is required before talking."

"You're right about that, cowboy." She turned to Reed. "It might be good for you to write that fact down. Remember, I'm always packing." She patted the side of her jacket where her pistol was.

"So am I, Chicago." He turned his waist to show off his own weapon of choice, which was holstered and attached to a leather belt around him. "So am I."

"Me, too, bro." Sawyer said. "That's two against one. Might be smart to listen to the lady and keep your morning motormouth in check, if you know what's good for you."

Reed snorted. "Okay, but we are getting up before the sun comes up. I want to see what morning sunshine looks like on her gorgeous face."

She shook her head. "Do those kind of lines work for you often?"

He grinned. "That's a new one, sweetheart. You tell me."

Sawyer glared at him. "You gotta control yourself. Jason asked us to help Nicole. Keep that in mind."

She couldn't stop herself from smiling. The playfulness and yes, even the lustiness of Reed got to her, as did the seriousness and gentleness of Sawyer. The brothers weren't quite polar opposites but not far from it either.

"Well?" Reed motioned her inside. "Let's give you the whole tour. Should take about ten seconds."

She stepped inside and was shocked to see such an orderly room. Nothing was out of place. How could it be the home of two bachelors? Then the thought hit her. *Maybe they're not single.* It seemed unlikely, but it was still possible. She hadn't asked them and they hadn't asked her. Neither of them wore a wedding ring but that didn't mean much. They were cowboys, working men. Jewelry didn't seem to fit into their line of work.

Her granddad had never worn a ring either, though he'd been married to her grandmother for many years. He always said jewelry belonged on two kinds of men—pimps and thugs. Granddad was from the old school of chauvinism, though he'd been her most staunch supporter when she decided to join the force. Had he lived, who knew how much more evolved he might've become.

"Chicago, you still with us or have you drifted off somewhere in your pretty head?" Reed asked.

"Just taking in your design sense. Don't rush me." Nothing was out of place. It was tidy and dust-free, which had to be quite a task indeed. "Either of you have girlfriends? Guys don't keep places this clean normally."

"We're far from normal." Reed grinned. "Would you be jealous if we did?"

He was such a flirt. "I'll take that as a 'no' to the girlfriend question."

"You like our place?" Sawyer asked.

She nodded. A leather sofa filled one side of the small room. On the other side, an enormous flat-screen television screamed that men decorated the space. A black cast-iron stove sat in one corner of the room, adding to the rustic feel of the place. The floors were made of beautiful hardwoods. The walls were logs, which were left rounded here in the inside just like on the outside. "Where's the kitchen? The bathroom? The bedrooms?"

Reed smiled and pointed to the stove in the corner. "That's the kitchen."

"You're kidding." A stove? After seeing it from the outside, she hadn't expected much, but she'd thought they would at least have a refrigerator.

"Nope."

So much for them having women in their lives. No way would any female put up with that. "What about a sink? Washing dishes?"

Reed pointed to the rear of the cabin. "See those two doors on the back wall, Chicago?"

"Yes."

"Power outages are common up here." Reed set her bag down on the floor. "The one on the right leads to the backyard. We chose to put in a hand water pump for our well."

Rustic doesn't even begin to describe this place. "What about freezing temperatures? Isn't that a problem here?"

"We built an insulated enclosure around it," Reed continued. "Dishes, laundry, bathing. It's all done out there."

She felt her eyes grow as big as saucers. "The sheriff wasn't kidding about this place being off the grid, was he?"

"No, Nicole." Sawyer put his hand on her shoulder. "We'll do our best to make things comfortable for you. Sorry about this. Our sister is the only woman who has ever been up here before."

Reed shrugged. "I hadn't thought about how this might seem to you. Sorry. Erica has never even spent a single night here."

The sudden softening in both of them caught her off guard. "It's okay. I'm not like most women. I can make this work. What about sleeping arrangements?" she asked, though nervous to hear what they would say.

"The door on the left is my bedroom," Sawyer answered, causing her nerves to swing into high gear. "Reed sleeps on the sofa sleeper out here. We always planned to put a second bedroom on the house at some point, but we've been focusing our extra cash on buying land."

No time like the present to get all the cards on the table. "What is your plan for tonight?"

Reed smirked. "What kind of guys do you think we are?"

She gulped. "I didn't mean that."

He laughed. "Too bad, because that's exactly the kind of guys we can be."

"Damn it, Reed. Stop teasing her." Sawyer turned to her, his face so tender and sweet. "You get the bedroom. One of us will sleep on the couch and the other in the chair."

"I call the sofa, bro. It's mine anyway. Of course that depends on what Chicago wants. Me out here or me in there with her," Reed said, once again reminding her of a sexy trickster. "The nights can get quite cold at this elevation, even in the summer. My body gives off more heat than you can imagine."

"Does it?" Just thinking about how the sexy, muscular cowboy's body would feel next to hers sent a whole bunch of shivers through her body.

"Well? What do you think about my offer, sweetheart?" Reed's blue eyes sparkled with mischief.

"Does the door have a lock?" she asked.

He sent her a toothy smile. "No."

"Damn it, stop teasing her. I swear I'm going to bust your chops if you don't start acting right, Reed." Sawyer pointed to the chair by the wood stove. "You can take that into the bedroom and prop it up against the knob. Will that work for you?"

"Yes," she said, though a wicked part of her didn't seem to agree. Images of being held by Reed floated in her mind, warming her up to a nice, toasty level. "Where should I put my things?"

Both cowboys' faces softened.

Reed spoke first. "In our mother's wardrobe."

"It's in the bedroom, Nicole," Sawyer added.

She remembered Reed talking about his mother down in Destiny. The sadness in his eyes was the same as now. Sawyer's green eyes held similar grief. Was this a family heirloom? Something they'd brought here to honor her?

Nicole thought about asking about their mom but decided against it. Opening up a dialog with them would certainly end up going both ways. They would answer her questions but then would ask her some of their own—some about her own mom. No way she wanted to go down that bitter road again, and certainly not with Reed and Sawyer. They seemed kind, honest, and generous, but they were still strangers to her. Best to keep them at arm's length.

"The wardrobe will be just fine."

Chapter Six

Reed felt like his heart was going to beat out of his chest. Just being near Nicole was impacting him in ways he'd never felt before. "You drove in from Illinois this morning, right?"

She nodded.

He turned to Sawyer. "I bet she wouldn't mind a bath, and before you say anything, just hear me out."

His brother's eyes narrowed. "Okay. Go on."

Moving his attention back to the raven-haired, curvy police officer, his dick stood up in his jeans and saluted. "Are you like most women where you would prefer a bath to a shower?"

"Yes, but it doesn't matter. I can make do." Her long lashes were mesmerizing, her brown eyes beguiling, and her lush lips mouthwatering. But it was much more than her body that held him captive. It was Nicole. Everything about her drew him in deeper and that wasn't good, not one fucking bit. By her very presence here in the cabin, his and Sawyer's castle, everything he'd known about the world seemed to be on the line.

"I know you can make do. You're the most self-reliant woman I've ever met." But he could sense in her a need to be cared for, to be possessed, to be dominated, and that made it all the harder for him to remain detached and emotionless. "We have a shower attached to the well house. We attach a garden hose to the faucet on the pump and to a line that feeds to the shower on the other side of the wall outside. The problem is the water is icy cold even this time of year."

"I'll manage."

"You don't have to manage, Chicago. We also have a tub that we put on the back porch during the winter. Even Reed and I can't stand the well water temperature then and have to take baths. We'll warm the water for you on the stove and fill up the tub."

She sighed. "I'm not sure taking a bath is a good idea. That's too much work."

"Let us worry about that. Trust me, you will love it." He turned back to Sawyer. "Let's fire up the stove and get the hot water going."

"You do that. I'll get the tub and bring it into the bedroom where she can have some privacy."

Damn, he knew Sawyer wanted to get a look at more of Nicole just as much as he did but was taking the high road as usual. Unfortunately, he, too, believed the high road was the way to go with her…for now.

"Guys, this is too much. What kind of tub are you talking about?"

"It's only a metal tub. Easy to move," Sawyer said.

"Not full of water." Reed saw he'd hit the mark with his brother by the look on his face.

"That's it. I'll take my bath on the back porch like everyone else. I'm sure you have some sheets that could be pinned up to give me a little privacy. Besides, you told me I could trust you. Was that true or not?"

"It's obvious you've got spunk, Chicago." Hoping to get a reaction from her, Reed sent her a wicked wink. "Might be fun for us to try to get that in check."

She frowned, but he could also feel a hint of her intrigue. "If you think I'm into what goes on in that club of yours, you're barking up the wrong tree."

Sawyer glared at him. "We'll use sheets, Nicole. I'll handcuff my brother if necessary to make sure you have the privacy you want."

"I'll behave. I promise." He didn't want to behave, but his brother was right. His dick didn't seem to want to stay in line though. He didn't dare close his eyes, knowing an image of Nicole naked underneath him would appear. But she was in trouble with the

Russian mafia. He was here to keep her safe. He needed to keep his hunger for her in check and stay focused on the task at hand. "Let's get Chicago's bath set up then. We only have a couple more hours of light left."

"Thanks. A bath does sound nice."

Sawyer nodded and started loading the stove with wood for the promised hot soak for Nicole.

Reed went out the back to get the metal tub to put on the porch as she went into the bedroom and shut the door.

How the hell was he going to get her out of his head? He wasn't sure, but he knew he must if he had any chance of steering clear of a certain disaster—his heart crushed. The plane crash that took his parents' lives nearly destroyed him. Sawyer and Erica, too. If he gave in to his desires for Nicole, he knew what would happen. She wasn't from Destiny. She was Chicago all the way. No way would she ever agree to stay here. So the best course of action he could take was to keep his desire for her under control. Of course, that didn't mean if opportunity knocked he wouldn't answer. That might be the best thing to happen. One tumble might cure him of these strange feelings for her. But what if they didn't?

He shook his head and stepped off the back porch to get the first buckets of water, when he spotted movement up the mountain to his left. Turning his head the direction of the motion, he pulled out his pistol and focused on the spot. Nothing. He didn't move. He'd learned long ago to trust his eyes. They hadn't failed. Continuing to stare at the area where he'd seen the activity for what seemed longer than it actually must've been, he finally saw the source of the disturbance up the mountain. It was Connie, his favorite big cat. Two sightings in one day? That was a record.

He remembered how excited Nicole had been when they'd seen the old girl in the middle of the road. Why couldn't he stop thinking about Nicole? He'd better figure out how soon or he might never be able to.

* * * *

Watching the steam rise from the water, Nicole stood by the metal tub on the back porch.

She grinned at the makeshift room of cotton sheets that Reed and Sawyer had fastened to the posts. The white fabric billowed slightly in the warm breeze. The table the brothers had placed next to the bath was filled with items they'd brought out here for her. It had a glass of iced tea, a plate of Hostess chocolate cupcakes, cloths and towels, shampoo and soap, and one of those iPod docking stations.

They'd even folded a big white cloth towel on the edge where her head would be once she got into the tub to make her more comfortable.

"Thank you so much for this," she told them. "I'm all set. If you'll be so kind as to leave, I can get undressed and into this inviting tub."

"One more thing, Chicago." Reed placed three birthday candles into one of the cupcakes. Then he lit them.

She was curious why he'd done that. "This isn't my birthday. That's in April, which has already passed."

"Good to know, but that's not what this is for, sweetheart," Reed said. "We don't want you thinking we're barbarians. A woman likes candles with a good soak, right?"

The twinkle in his eyes made her grin. "Yes."

"These are the only kind we have in the cabin. We have some lanterns we use when the electricity goes out, but he didn't think that would be the same," Sawyer added. "I told him it would be better to nix the candle idea and bring out a lantern instead."

"No. I think it's sweet."

Reed smiled. "Told you."

"Yes, you did," Sawyer said, also smiling. "Let's give the lady her privacy."

As they walked out of the space, she held her change of clothes and gun in her hands and listened to the country music coming out of the docking station's speakers.

Even though she'd lived her whole life in the Windy City, she'd been a fan of that genre of music just like her granddad. Lots of his fellow officers had teased him about it. She grinned recalling one time she'd heard him rebuff them for their jokes in his thick Chicago accent. "I was going ta take one of you ta see da Bearsss wid me. You forgot dat I won doze tickets on the fiddy-yard line from the radio station didn't ya? I'm gonna take Nicky instead—*at*." It was always funny how Granddad had often ended his sentences with extra words, mostly prepositions, that didn't quite make sense.

God, she missed him. Suddenly, the old guilt swept through her. For the first year after he'd been diagnosed, she'd done her best. The next year—and the last of his life—she'd done her worst.

Sawyer paused, the sheet he was pushing aside still in his hand. His left eyebrow shot up. "Everything okay?"

She was normally better at keeping her poker face on. She placed her clean clothes and gun on the table by the tub. "It's perfect. Thank you."

"We'll be inside if you need anything, Chicago." Reed's voice came from the other side of the cloth dividers.

"All you have to do is yell," Sawyer instructed. "We'll leave the door propped open so we can hear you."

"Thank you. I will," she said.

Sawyer nodded and lowered the sheet, leaving her in the outdoor retreat they'd created for her. She listened to their departing footsteps as they entered the cabin. With a big sigh, she plunged her fingertips below the water's surface. The temperature was just right, nice and warm. She looked up into the pale blue sky, which was populated with puffy white clouds. Chicago had a few days with this kind of sky—but just a few—and could only be really viewed best on Lake Shore Drive, miles from where she and her grandfather had lived. There, up above the mid-rise buildings, only a strip of the heavens could be seen by the masses below.

She thought about pinching herself to make sure all of this was real. How long had it been since anyone waited on her?

Never.

Reed and Sawyer had a rugged charm that was compelling. Wondering what it would be like if they didn't keep their promise and leave her alone, she felt a naughty shiver shoot through her body. But despite Reed's wicked talk and Sawyer's steamy stares, she believed they would be true to their word and give her privacy.

Chapter Seven

Reed sat on the sofa next to Sawyer. They'd popped in a movie, his all-time favorite John Wayne flick *True Grit*, but strangely it wasn't holding his attention. Something else was. Actually *someone* else was, and she was taking a bath on the back porch right now. Nicole was more than beautiful—she was drop-dead gorgeous. Tough, too. She had more guts than most men he knew.

God, this wasn't good.

Sure, one day he and Sawyer would choose a woman to share. He'd known that his whole life. Destiny was special that way. Actually, it was the women who were special that way. A lone mortal man couldn't even come close to giving what these angels deserved. He'd seen what a loving family could be in his mother and two dads. Dad Gene and Dad Gilbert had doted on their mom with such joyous abandon. It had been such a loving sight to behold. Before the plane crash he'd even believed he and Sawyer would one day find a woman to love. *Before.* But he knew the risk now that letting your heart take the lead over your head would do. Pain, crushing and horrific. He'd been fifteen when his parents had died. He wasn't a child anymore. He didn't want to ever risk that kind of hurt again. Ever. There were two people in his life that he allowed himself to love. His brother and sister—Sawyer and Erica. There wasn't room for anyone else. Once Sawyer and he were ready to settle down, he would agree to a new wife so that they could add to the Coleman name by making babies. He would be happy to have fondness for the woman they chose, but not love. Love meant ceding his control.

But why the fuck couldn't he stop thinking about *her*? Every second since she'd been with him and Sawyer—from the moment she'd walked into the playroom in Phase Four to now, on the back porch behind those goddamn sheets washing her naked body—his mind wouldn't back down and latch onto logic. *Damn it, I need to get a fucking grip.*

He refocused his attention back on the television. The movie was at the part where John Wayne's character was on the horse looking down at Robert Duval's character—Ned Pepper, who was calling him fat.

Now, I can settle into this.

"What are we going to do about Nicole?" Sawyer asked, jerking him out of his resolve to concentrate on the movie instead of their guest.

"What about her?" he snapped.

"She's stubborn. I'm thinking we can get her to stay put another day, maybe two, but no more. She's in real danger. You know Jason. He wouldn't have asked us to keep an eye on her if she wasn't. He's too practical and too by-the-book to do that normally."

"That's true. Jason doesn't veer from his convictions." The sheriff had a clear sense of right or wrong and he'd suffered from his unbending nature. He'd lost Phoebe because of it, and his brothers had never really forgiven him. The four of them were beginning what looked to be a serious relationship when Jason, just a deputy at the time, caught Shane with drugs. Mitchell and Lucas had begged their brother to go easy on Shane, but Jason had refused. His hard-boiled testimony got the book thrown at Shane, who received the most severe sentence allowable for a first-time offender. Phoebe hadn't been able to forgive Jason for sending her brother to jail.

Sawyer shook his head. "I can't believe the Russians might be coming back to Destiny after all that happened with the Stones."

Remembering Jason's words about Nicole being in the center of a deadly mess got Reed's guilt to crawl out of the shadows and chilled his blood. He'd been so wrapped up in his own crap, making sure he didn't fall for her, that he'd forgotten why she was here in the first place. That was what happened when someone like him let his emotions get the better of him. Time to kick logic, which he *could* understand, into a full-on gallop.

"She needs us, Reed."

"Of course. That's why she's here."

Sawyer shook his head. "I'm not talking about you and I being her bodyguards. I'm talking about the hurt she's carrying. Can't you feel it every time you look at her? Her pain is deep and heavy. She's been carrying it for some time."

God, he never understood how Sawyer could see so deeply into people, especially women. But even this seemed more than his normal sixth-sense bullshit. "What are you talking about? ESP? You don't have it. We have a job to do and that's what I plan to do. Case closed."

Sawyer glared at him. "Damn it, Reed. Don't do this."

"Do what?"

"Fuck, you know what I mean. You're pulling back for some reason. Stop it."

"And you're jumping in with both feet, aren't you?" He had to try to snap Sawyer back to reality. "Need I remind you she's from Chicago, not Destiny? She has a life, a job, and who knows what else back there. She mentioned knowing what kind of club Phase Four was but that doesn't mean she's into BDSM or has the slightest notion what the life is really about."

Sawyer smiled. "I knew it. You're into her, too."

"Wrong," he lied. "You're no mind reader." But clearly Sawyer was. *Fuck.*

"Deny it all you want, bro. I can tell." Sawyer grabbed the remote and muted the movie. "You might be right though. She's not from here. Chicago might hold more for her than Destiny. All true. BDSM? That's always been your thing more than mine."

"Bullshit. Now who is lying?" Sawyer spent just as much time at the club as he did. "You enjoy it as much as I do."

"And you enjoy a revolving door of subs."

"So?" Reed liked to play. Why was that a problem?

"Why?" Sawyer asked.

"Why not?"

Sawyer sighed, clearly frustrated. "Stop answering my questions with questions, Reed. Why aren't you ready to settle down? I'm turning thirty in September. You'll be twenty-eight in June. Isn't it time to grow up?"

Why the hell was Sawyer pushing him on this topic? "If you already can read my mind, you tell me."

"I think you never got over our parents' death."

"And you and Erica did? Nice. Really nice," he said, hoping the sarcastic tone wasn't lost on Sawyer.

His brother shook his head. "No. I'll never really be over it, but I've healed. I've gone on. I want a future, one with a woman I can love like our dads loved Mom."

Reed closed his eyes, feeling every single day that had passed since the tragedy. Had it only been thirteen years ago? He would've sworn on the stand in the Swanson County Courthouse it had been twice, even three times that long. He felt every one of his years. "I want a wife, too."

"Are you sure about that?" Sawyer asked. "You can honestly say you're ready to settle down, to swear off the sea of subs we've had over the years for one woman for the rest of our lives?"

"You're talking about Nicole, aren't you?" Time for Reed to get his point across. Time to make sure Sawyer didn't fantasize about a life with Chicago. It just wasn't possible. "This isn't one of your 'Time to Grow Up' speeches. This is about her."

Sawyer shook his head "In part, yes, but not completely. Yes, I'm interested in her. I'm ready to get to know her better. More than a little, I must admit. She's like no other woman we've ever been with. But you're right. She's not from here. Convincing her to stay might prove impossible, though I suspect that if we take our time and get to know her better, we might actually succeed. You know you're a lot like Dad Gene, bro. Erica's more like Mom."

"And I suppose you're like Dad Gilbert?" Reed asked.

"I think so," Sawyer confirmed. "Remember, he could also read minds. Or have you forgotten that?"

"I don't forget anything." If only he could.

"I know."

"How is Erica like Mom?" God, Reed missed his mother.

Sawyer smiled. "Her humor is identical to Mom's. She can see good where others can't."

"Yeah. I agree, although she's not the same since the shooting at TBK. I think she's having a hard time getting over the guilt she feels for letting Felix into Eric and Scott's office." Reed was worried about her.

"I've noticed that, too." Sawyer sighed. "I wish Mom were here. She would know how to help Erica. I'll never forget how she used to smile and pull me into a hug when I was upset. Mom's eyes were so bright."

"Erica's got her eyes. She's looking more and more like Mom every day." In the drawer of his nightstand was a bottle of his mom's perfume. Whenever he found himself alone in the cabin, he would pull it out and inhale the fragrance to remind him of her.

Sawyer nodded.

Reed shook his head, trying to clear his mind. "God, I forgot how much you are like a woman."

"What do you mean?"

"You love talking about your feelings. Feelings are way overrated if you ask me."

Sawyer laughed. "Just like Dad Gene for sure."

"How so?" Reed thought Sawyer was right about the similarity he had with Dad Gene.

"Like you, he stuffed his emotions away. Of course he had them, plenty of them."

"How would you know that?"

"He told me." Sawyer seemed lost in his memories. "Remember the fishing trip I took with the dads when you had the flu the summer before the crash?"

"Of course." Reed had hated to miss the trip, but his mom had insisted he stay at home.

"Dad Gene took me aside and gave me *the talk*."

Reed laughed. "Weren't you a little old for that? You might've been a virgin but you knew about sex."

"I did, but it wasn't that talk. It was about how Dad Gene saw life. He was proud of us both already, but it was hard for him to tell us. You remember how he was."

"Yes, I do." And the similarities continued on in him. "Talking is overrated, too, if you ask me."

"I didn't, bro." Sawyer smiled, and then he looked him straight in the eyes. "You and I have always shared the beds of women together."

"True. If it weren't for me, you would've stayed a virgin your whole life, I'm betting."

Sawyer shrugged. "Maybe so. Our lifestyle is all I know. I can't even imagine any other way of being."

"Me, too." Reed felt overwhelmingly weary. He had to make him understand even if it ripped his own conscience in two. "But our lifestyle is considered aberrant and fringe on the outside and in Illinois—where she comes from."

Sawyer sighed. "True. All true."

God, he hated the look on his brother's face, the look of fading hope. He wished he could let himself risk it all, risk his heart, but he couldn't. He was already in way too deep with Nicole. Time to save himself and Sawyer from impending loss and pain.

"Yes, I'll settle down if you're ready, but we need to choose someone other than Nicole. Someone from Destiny—or from one of the many towns where people understand our ways like Bliss or Wilde, Nevada—not Chicago, Illinois."

* * * *

Slipping out of her clothes, Nicole thought about how long it had been since she'd been with a man. Any man. Over eighteen months. There were many good reasons why it had been such an extended dry spell for her. One, the few experiences she'd had were at best okay. Two, the men she'd been with were slam-bam-thank-you-ma'am kind of guys. The type of foreplay she'd been exposed to mainly consisted of sixty seconds of kissing, another sixty of breast massaging, sixty more of the guy stripping her of her clothes, and then sixty seconds of clumsy fingers touching her body. Four to five minutes tops before "magic time." Jerks. But the main reason for giving up on men altogether was it was better to be alone. Besides, sex didn't hold much of an appeal for her. She'd never understood what all the hoopla about sex was in the first place. It was either a myth society continued to perpetuate or she was certainly missing something.

Getting into the warm bath, she wondered if Reed and Sawyer would know how to help her to experience this so-called "orgasm."

For Christ's sake, get ahold of yourself, Nicole. I'm here for one reason and one reason only.

Even though the water felt surprisingly sinful on her skin, she vowed to herself to keep her thoughts under control. She decided to go ahead and wash her long hair. It would take a good deal of time to dry and even more to brush out, but she wasn't going anywhere tonight, thanks to Sheriff Wolfe and Henry's meddling.

She plunged beneath the surface, disturbing the warm liquid and drenching her locks. She took the plastic bottle of shampoo and squeezed out a generous portion of its contents in the palm of her hand. The gel's coconut fragrance, one of her favorites, seemed odd to her. Reed and Sawyer were beautifully unrefined. They seemed more suited to a no-nonsense shampoo like Head and Shoulders. She doubted they'd ever even heard the word "metrosexual" here in Northern Colorado. They were manly men. Cowboys. So how did this ill-matched milky-scented shampoo with conditioner make it to their back porch? Perhaps no woman had decorated the bachelor-motif cabin but that didn't mean there hadn't been women visitors other than their sister. A sudden stinging jealousy nipped at her insides. Would they lie to her about that? They had no reason to. That thought softened the harsh green she was feeling. Maybe the only female to come here was their sister.

Why do I even care? Good God, what's wrong with me?

She continued with her bath, washing her hair. After a good rinse, she grabbed one of the towels on the table and dried her dark strands. Once the bulk of the water was squeezed out, she wrapped her hair up in the towel. She took a cloth and began washing her skin. After her soothing cleanse, she curled her fingers around the glass of iced tea. The brothers had added lemon and just the right amount of sugar. The cool drink on her tongue and the warm water on her skin created one of the most relaxing moments she'd ever experienced. Placing the glass back on the table, she closed her eyes as her favorite Lee Ann Womack song began to play. Listening to the lyrics, another vision of Reed and Sawyer filled her mind, but this time she was part of the dream, dancing blissfully between them.

Reed held her hand and spun her around the floor, his stunning blue eyes reaching deep inside her. "Chicago, you're fantastic. I'm so glad you agreed to dance with us."

Sawyer took his turn with her, showing off his dancing skills, too, capturing her attention with his lush manly lips. What would it feel like to have them on her skin? On her nipples? Between her thighs? A tiny moan left her mouth, as her need expanded deep inside her.

Anxious and excited, she felt her heart race in her chest. Her knees buckled, and she would've hit the floor if Sawyer and Reed hadn't been holding her between them. God, it was the most wonderful place to be. Something amazing was filling every atom in the room and beyond. The air sparkled with pinpoints of light and smelled of honeysuckle. Even her cowboys' skin sparkled like diamonds in this misty expanse. She felt giant tears of joy in her eyes. So long she'd struggled. So long she'd been alone. Was this what happiness felt like?

A change of music to a slower tempo made her body burn even hotter. Sawyer pulled her in close, taking her breath away. Without so much as even a hint of jealousy, he passed her off to Reed. The mischievous brother held her tight against his rock-hard torso, moving her around the heavenly room.

God, she loved being here with these wonderful cowboys, feeling safe and secure. Loved.

Reed and Sawyer lifted her up into their arms and the dance floor vanished and in its place was a dreamy room with a big comfy bed in the center of the space. Her heart fluttered in her chest as they placed her tenderly on the fluffy comforter. Reed and Sawyer got onto the bed, positioning her between them. She lowered her head to the silk-covered pillow. The bed began to slowly spin and rise up. As they started caressing her, warmth filled her body. Her eyes softened. Tingles spread through her. Her senses had never been so alive, so heightened.

"Chicago," Reed said tenderly. "We're here for you."

"We'll always be here," Sawyer chimed in.

She believed them, trusted them, and wanted them. She felt accepted, desired, and she no longer felt alone.

Reed's fingertips stroked her back, igniting every nerve ending inside her.

Being between the two sexy wranglers made her hesitations vanish and her instincts break through. Suddenly, both of them were stripped off their clothing. She felt her eyes grow as big as saucers as she gazed at the perfect male physiques right in front of her. She looked down at her own body, which was magically free of attire, too.

Normally, she would feel too exposed and fearful to let anyone see her this way, but not now, not with Reed and Sawyer.

"Hey, Chicago." Reed's hands slid along the sides of her neck. She could feel the heat of his and Sawyer's bodies next to her. "How are you feeling?"

"Amazing," she replied, shivering as twenty fingers feathered her skin. Why was it so easy to let them touch her so intimately? Because this wasn't real. This was a dream. A deliciously wicked dream. Here, she could be herself. A woman.

Her grandfather had done his best bringing her up, but without a female influence in her life, it was no wonder she'd been more tomboy than anything. Shaking that image of her at the station hadn't ever happened either. Showing the world a tough exterior was as natural to her as breathing. Now, with Reed and Sawyer, she could be her true self, a feminine woman who didn't mind being treated as such. She was starting to think of these sexy cowboys as much more than recently appointed bodyguards. The way they looked at her, eating her up with their eyes, sent shocking shivers through her body.

What would it mean to her to give in to their wicked offer of a ménage à trois? What would happen after they had her? Did the future matter at all? This was her dream, her fantasy. Anything was possible.

"Sweetheart, how does this feel?" Sawyer rubbed her shoulders, releasing the tension there.

"I love how you touch me," she confessed.

Reed smiled, making her tingle between her thighs and causing her pussy to dampen. "If you think his fingers are good you tell me how mine feel, Chicago." He feathered his digits down her arms, causing goose bumps to pop up. "Well?"

"Wonderful, cowboy. Your hands have magic in them."

"Damn right," he said with a laugh.

It was good to let go, to feel, to be a woman. Keeping up appearances, remaining a tough cop, tamping down her emotions, all of it necessary but also so tiring. Being intimate after so long was deliciously devastating to her. She needed this in the worst way. She let go of the worries about the station, about Henry, about the investigation, about the missing persons report. In these men's arms she felt new sensations, and she could just be herself.

Sawyer was a gentleman, always gaging her comfort level. Sexy as hell. Kind to a fault. And mouthwateringly tempting.

Reed was a devil, plain and simple. He clearly enjoyed trying to make her blush, and more than once, he'd succeeded—something that rarely happened. Blushing cops didn't do well on the streets of Chicago. His grin crushed, and his blue eyes devastated.

Both men had agreed to protect her, and the truth of the matter was she was thrilled they had. Gun-toting muscled cowboys were her bodyguards. What woman wouldn't love that? The sheriff, with the help of Henry, had forced her into a corner—a corner that included Reed and Sawyer. She'd given in quickly, and now, she was so glad she had.

"You're so beautiful." Reed captured her with his wicked gaze. Had she ever seen a more beautiful man in her whole life? No. His wavy, blond hair begged for her fingers, and she willingly complied.

"I don't know about that," she said as her fingertips touched his golden strands. "I'm pretty average at best. More tomboy than girl, if you ask me."

"Stop." Reed's face darkened. "You. Are. Beautiful."

As he pressed his lips to hers and Sawyer continued stroking her back, she felt fresh tears sting her eyes.

"We'll never let you go, Nicole." Sawyer's words wrapped themselves around her entire being. God, how she wanted what he said to be true, to be real. An incurable loneliness drowned her night after night. Would it ever end? Here, with Reed and Sawyer, she could feel a light breaking through into her darkness. Maybe it would only last for a little while, but it would be the relief she needed from her suffering.

Sawyer's hand moved down to the curve of her hip while Reed's cupped her breast. She was cradled between them and loving every second of it. Her head was swimming from desire and need. She was feverish for pleasure. Her whole body felt like it was spinning, open and ready to receive whatever they had in store for her.

Reed brushed his lips with hers, a tender caress, a kiss with the promise of more. As their noses touched, she felt like she was floating on air, in the clouds, spinning in their arms.

Sawyer slowly and gently kissed her neck. She could feel his tongue sweep across her skin, filling her with agonizing need. Her toes curled as a hot sensation that began in her belly spread out through the rest of her body, finally settling between her thighs. She was getting so very wet.

Their cowboys' kisses came slowly, pressing here and there, dotting her entire body with their seductive lips.

She shuddered as Reed's tongue circled her nipples, causing them to ache and harden. Sawyer's lips skated down her back all the way to her ass. When she felt him lick her there, a sea of sensations flooded into her, opening her up, making her ready to receive them in the most intimate way. As their fingers and lips roamed across her skin, her desire to have them inside her body grew and grew to a maddening level.

Reed moved down her body until she could feel his hot breath on her mound. "I want to taste you, Chicago." He grabbed her thighs and spread them wide. His greedy tongue lapped up her cream. Her hands shot to the back of his head, as if they had minds of their own, pulling him in closer. Her body's need was too much to bear. She needed relief so badly. Instead they turned up the heat inside her. Sawyer's mouth swallowed one of her breasts, making her wonderfully dizzy. Reed's fingers rubbed her pussy as his tongue hit her clit. She heard herself whimper, brought on by the tremendous tingles ripping through her body, one after another after another.

Reed's thirst seemed unending as his hands and mouth continued their assault on her pussy. Sawyer's, too, as his conquered every inch of her upper half, breasts, neck, arms, tummy, and more.

"Time to show this beautiful creature what we can do for her." Reed's lusty tone caused her insides to violently pulse again and again.

Suddenly, she was no longer on the bed but in their arms, pinned between them. She could feel their cocks lined up against her body— Reed's to her pussy and Sawyer's to her ass. This was what they meant to do to her just like she hoped they would. They wanted to claim her, all of her, and with everything inside her, that was what she wanted, too.

Reed smiled and then stuck out his tongue until it hit the tip of her nose. She found it odd that he would do that. Then he began licking her nose, which was even stranger.

"Reed, what are you doing?" she asked, reaching up to push him away.

When her fingertips touched not Reed, but something with tiny legs on her face, she opened her eyes and screamed.

Chapter Eight

Nicole opened her eyes and swatted at the thing on her nose that had pulled her from the dream she was having about Sawyer and Reed. What was it? She looked down the bridge of her nose but her eyes didn't seem to want to focus. Her mind was still fuzzy from her recent doze in the tub.

Suddenly, she heard footsteps and then the sheets fell to the ground. Sawyer and Reed stood there with their guns drawn and ready for whatever assailant she faced.

"You okay, Chicago?" Reed's worried eyes locked on her.

"It's a–a…"

"A what?" Sawyer asked, looking around the porch.

And then the monster came into view. "It's a moth," she confessed, shocked and embarrassed.

"What do we do now?" Reed said, aiming his gun at the winged insect now rising into the air. "Do you want me to shoot it?"

Coming out of the water and to her feet, she laughed, grabbing the towel they'd left for her and wrapping it around her body. "Now do you believe me when I say I'm a seasoned cop?"

Both men cracked up, and that fueled her hysterics. It felt good to laugh, to let go, to be happy.

She felt herself shivering and looked down. The towel didn't cover much. The sudden heat in her cheeks reminded her of that fact.

"Here's another towel, Chicago." She looked up and into Reed's steady gaze, which was fixed on her eyes. "The temperature drops fast in the mountains this late in the day."

As her giggles softened, she took the welcomed longer towel and wrapped it around her body. Reed was supposed to be the lustier one of the two cowboys. At least that was what he'd consistently been like since she'd met him. "A damn moth. Oh my God."

A new round of happy shrieks left her lips, causing them to all nearly fall to the floor again.

"We'll always save you, Chicago," Reed said, his tone taking on a serious note.

"Thank you." Lost in the moment of his sweetness, she couldn't remember ever being so relaxed, so calm. It wouldn't have happened without Reed and Sawyer. They'd helped her get to this wonderful state. "I don't know how I would've survived that beast without you." The cowboys smiled and she leaned forward and pressed her lips to Reed's and then to Sawyer's. These men had brought out a side of her she'd never experienced.

Again, she shivered but this time it wasn't from being chilled—quite the opposite. This time it was from her insides warming up. She turned her attention back to Reed and Sawyer. They were looking at her with potent stares. *Oh God, why did I do that?*

"Thank you for the sweet kiss, Chicago." Reed cupped her chin. "But now that I've tasted those gorgeous lips of yours, I want more."

His mouth came crashing into hers. Her kiss had been meant as a sweet thank-you. His was something else entirely. He clearly intended to take charge here, to flood her with his will. He tasted warm and so very manly. Heat spread through her as his tongue traced the line between her lips and then pushed in—into her mouth. Her toes curled and her heart swelled in her chest. When his arms came around her, a tingle spread through her. Such rock-solid muscles pressing against her soft flesh reminded her she was a woman, feminine and vulnerable. Even in this state of vulnerability, she felt protected by him. His lusty kiss went on and on, and she began to feel woozy.

This is real. This isn't a dream.

She could feel his rugged hands on her shoulders, sending quakes through her body from his fingertips. She'd been drowning for years, flooded with guilt and loneliness. For the first time in a very long time she could stop trying so hard and just be. God, it felt so good, so wonderful, so…there just weren't words to describe what she was feeling.

Reed released her lips for a moment and pulled her hair out of the towel she'd wrapped it in. She looked at his face, so incredibly handsome. Feeling his hands on her back took her breath away.

"Sawyer, you have to taste her lips. They're delicious." Reed took a step back.

Sawyer moved in front of her. The sweet gentleman cowboy she'd come to know in him was gone. Now, he looked more savage than civilized, more dangerous than sweet. His hands caught her hair and the little tug he gave her locks caused her breath to catch in her chest. "Yes, I must."

He leaned down and kissed her fully on the mouth. It wasn't a gentle brush of his mouth against hers by any definition. There was clearly hunger in his lips and tongue, deep and hot. Her body's reaction startled her. Never had she gotten so wet so fast, and especially not from a kiss. Her clit began to throb steadily. She felt so very warm as Sawyer's domination of her mouth continued. As he pulled her in closer, his tongue swept past her lips.

Suddenly, Sawyer shoved his arms under her knees and hauled her up his massive frame. Nicole was thrilled at how light she felt in his hold. She placed her forehead on his chest and wrapped her arms around his neck. As he carried her back into the cabin, Reed followed behind.

Still groggy from the lazy bath, she closed her eyes, relishing the indulgent haze.

Sawyer held her tight. "You're beautiful, sweetheart. So fucking beautiful." He spoke like she was a goddess and he was her worshiper.

"Thank you," she said, feeling the prick of happy tears in her eyes. "You both have been so sweet to me."

"Sweet?" Reed said. "I've never been accused of that before, Chicago." Then his laugh that followed his words reached into her, filling her with warmth and tiny quakes.

Even though the guilt and demons of her past seemed so very far away from here, they were still present in the back of her mind. Their voices, now muted, still mocked and taunted her to turn back from this path of pleasure, saying she didn't deserve this—ever. And there was still the business of the missing persons report issue. The sheriff might have sidetracked her for a day or two, but no more. She needed to get back on the case to help Henry, despite his good-intentioned betrayal. She looked into Sawyer's green eyes, and then at Reed's blue ones. Their dual intensity was mind-boggling and body-warming. She wanted them. They wanted her.

As Sawyer lowered her onto the mattress, she felt almost as though it was floating like the one in the dream. Or was it just her body that was soaring above the covers? Hovering mattress or buoyant body didn't seem to change the fact that her bathtub dream had miraculously come into being in the here and now, in the flesh of two sexy cowboys, from her imagination into her reality.

Sawyer moved onto the bed next to her, skating his fingertips along her arms. "I want you to think of this room as a safe haven, baby. Tonight is about you. Okay?"

She nodded, tingling from head to toe.

Reed took off his shirt revealing his wickedly hot chest. "We're going to give you so much pleasure in this bed, Chicago, your body and mind will be totally blown. Mark my words."

I guess the case can wait until tomorrow.

"Kiss me, baby." Sawyer leaned in, and she let her arms circle his neck once again. She pressed her mouth to his. As he whetted their kiss, sending his hungry tongue past her lips, she inhaled his manly scent of leather and gunpowder with the slightest note of steel. Still humid from her recent watery doze, her pussy's ache returned and multiplied. Everything inside her seemed to be burning divinely.

When their kiss ended, she looked over at Reed, who was now completely devoid of clothing and holding a box of condoms. Her heart thudded in her chest like a racehorse. A sharp, logical mind would most definitely hit the brakes on this course, but her mind was neither at the moment. Right or wrong, she wanted them to take her, to claim her, to make her feel like never before, to help her forget.

"Don't forget the lube, Reed." Sawyer's lips crushed against hers once again, blasting her need into the stratosphere.

With one cowboy kissing her, the other removed the towel from her body. She could feel Reed's lips on the back of her neck. In a flash, the brothers shuffled her between them, switching positions. Reed was next to her on the bed, kissing her, and Sawyer was stripping off his clothes.

When Reed pushed the hair out of her eyes, she chewed on her lower lip, trying to keep herself from moaning. The sensations they were creating in her were more than she'd ever felt before. Hot. Electric. Massive.

Reed kissed her, tangling his tongue with hers. Every nerve inside her seemed alive and on fire. Feeling Reed's thick, hard cock against her naked thigh sparked a renewed burn in her throbbing clit. She closed her eyes as his lips moved from her mouth to her neck, pelting her with hot kisses. She was having trouble catching her breath as Sawyer's tongue traced the center of her back and down her spine. Their dual mouth assault was sending her higher and higher, hotter and hotter. Her walls were not only down, but were crumbling into rubble and dust by these men. Why? What was it about them that pushed her forward for more? Everything. Their rugged charm and honest desire had taken hold of her. Though she'd been careful not to let her intrigue of them show at the club in Destiny, she had been captivated from the beginning. Now, she was completely mesmerized by them. Reed and Sawyer had an impact on her like no men she'd ever known.

"I shouldn't do this," she said, as the old painful memories began to creep into her consciousness again. *I don't deserve this.*

Reed's all-consuming blue stare made her blink. He moved his gaze to Sawyer. She turned to her other cowboy and looked into his knowing eyes. It was as if he could see into her most secret places.

Sawyer smiled and cupped her chin. He didn't say anything but turned to Reed. Something unspoken seemed to pass between them. Then their joint and confident attention landed right on her.

"Not only do you deserve this, Nicole, you need this." Sawyer's kindness took her breath away.

Giving in to her emotions got her in trouble. Always. But she didn't want to get them back under control now even though she knew she should. She wanted to feel again, really feel. These men were opening her up and she just couldn't bring herself to stop them. Still, wasn't it important to make them understand? Didn't they have a right to know how screwed up she was? "You should know something about me before we do this."

Reed's comforting smile caused her heart to leap in her chest. "I know all I need to know, Chicago."

Sawyer stroked her hair. "Whatever demons you carry, sweetheart, don't matter to us. We want you to have pleasure."

Their sweet words made her want to cry. No one had ever made her feel so wanted in her whole life.

Reed kissed her shoulder. "You've had it hard, haven't you?"

She held back her tears by blinking. "No more than most, I suppose."

"Not true, baby," Sawyer said. "Let us make things easier for you, at least for tonight. We can handle everything."

She looked from one brother to the other, shocked to see immeasurable tenderness in their eyes. It was too much, too powerful, too possessive even. "I'm not trying to be difficult," she said, though knowing that was exactly what she was being. She had to. She'd always taken care of herself, good or bad, right or wrong. As much as she'd like to think of this as just sex, it wouldn't be. That was something she was certain of. "I'm just saying it might be better to slow roll this, don't you think?"

"Slow is fun sometimes, but I'm not sure that's what you want, Nicole." That was the first time Reed had called her by her actual name, and it made her shiver with delight, though when he called her "Chicago" that also never failed to make her tingle. His fingertips ran down her trembling arm. "Do you really want us to stop?"

"No," she said, hearing the whisper of desire in her own voice.

Reed smiled, and she saw fire ignite in his blue eyes, making her feel wonderfully vulnerable.

Surrounded by the heat of his and Sawyer's bodies, she felt her need expand inside her, heat ripping through every inch of her insides. She closed her eyes and moaned as each of them kissed her tingling skin on opposite sides of her neck. Reed's hand cupped her breasts and Sawyer's skated down her side and over her abdomen. Their cocks pressed against her thighs causing her breath to catch in her chest and heat shivers to go up and down her spine. Every nerve seemed to sizzle and spark as their mouths and hands worked her body into a state of frenzy. She could feel electrified currents coming online through her, from her neck to her breasts down her belly to her dampening pussy.

Reed moved from her neck to her breast, a hungry manly hum vibrating through his lips to her tingling nipple. "You're killing me, Chicago. Do you know that?" And then he captured her taut bit of flesh between his teeth, delivering the perfect amount of pressure.

"Ohhh." *You're killing me, too.* She looked over at Sawyer, who was sliding one of his hands over her thighs and the other through her hair. His eyes were hooded with desire.

"You're safe here, Nicole. With us." Even Sawyer's words stirred her beyond measure.

Reed's warm breath on her nipple made her heart race even more.

Everything inside her was on fire, and she sent her hands, one for each cowboy, into their manly locks.

Reed tilted his head up and fixed his eyes to hers. "You like?"

"God, yes," she confessed, unable to hold back anything from them at the moment.

He moved up her body until his lips were hovering above hers. "So do I, Chicago. So do I." Then he pressed them hard on her mouth, keeping one hand on her breast. His rough fingers tenderly massaged her chest as he forced her lips apart with his hungry tongue. Everything in her swelled—her lips, her breasts, her nipples, her clit…everything. She felt light and heavy at the same time. The delicious heat they were stoking in her created fresh tingling sensations that made her squirm. Reed swallowed her moans, and then he began pinching her nipples, one after another. She'd never felt like this before, so filled with want and desire. Intimacy had never been so…so powerful and crushing. Sucking on Reed's tongue, she moved her hands from their thick hair down their necks to their muscled chests. God, they were built. Years of riding horses and working on this ranch had sculpted their perfect masculine bods.

Sawyer's fingers moved closer and closer to her most intimate place, her pussy. "Please touch me," she whimpered, shocked at her lack of control and her overwhelming need. "I'm dying to be touched."

Had she ever been so honest with anyone before? No. She'd never allowed herself to be. Couldn't. But with Reed and Sawyer she was ready to open up and be exposed, which was thrilling and stunning, too. Their beauty was breathtaking and their tenderness was staggering. They were strong men, wonderful and passionate. Something told her they were keeping themselves in check, reining in their hunger and thirst for her. Still, she caught rare glimpses in their gorgeous eyes of something deliciously wicked and overwhelming. It was like she'd been frozen for years, stuck even, but Reed and Sawyer were melting away the hesitation, the suffering, and the doubt with their intoxicating caresses.

When she felt Sawyer's hands finally touch her pussy, she gasped.

An aching surge of sensations shot through her body. She was wetter than she'd ever been before in her life. Reed returned to sucking on her nipples, leaving behind her swollen and throbbing lips. Her breasts swelled from his light touch. She wanted more, so much more. She felt woozy and vulnerable between them. When Sawyer circled her clit with his thumb, her pussy clenched again and again.

"Oh God. I–I have never…I can't…" She was having trouble concentrating. The new sensual sensations were ripping through her like wildfire.

"Enjoy this, Nicole. Every touch is for you." Sawyer's tone had an edge to it. Was he struggling to keep control? "Fuck, I can't wait to be inside you." Yes. He was struggling. What would happen if he gave completely in to his lust? A wicked, apprehensive shiver rolled through her at the possibility.

Reed sucked on one of her nipples and rolled the other one between his thumb and forefinger. His bite and pinch worked together to increase her hurting need to a level that was next to unbearable. But his wonderful torture continued, going on and on, raising her higher and higher. She'd never wanted anything like she wanted Reed and Sawyer right now. It was strong and even frightening in a way. She'd faced dangerous men before, but these cowboys were a different kind of danger, and the unfamiliar sensations they were awakening inside her were so very intense.

She'd had sex before but this was a level of intimacy she'd never known. Surrendering to them tonight seemed so natural, so right. The weight of her world was being lifted, if only for now, from her shoulders. This was what it meant to be in the moment, to let go, to feel.

"I can't stand waiting any longer." Sawyer's lusty words filled her with white-hot hunger. "I've got to taste you, baby." He moved down her body, separating her thighs with his firm hands and positioning his hot mouth right above her navel until she could feel the heat of his breath on her skin. He decorated her abdomen with hot, manly kisses.

Then he moved down, slowly, a fraction of an inch at a time. Closer. Closer. Closer. God, her urgent need grew and grew and still his advance to her pussy was agonizingly unhurried.

She whimpered and clawed at Reed's chest. "Please. Oh please." Her own carnality surprised her. Had she ever been so lusty in her life? No. Never.

Reed lapped at her chest with no hesitation, and every lick ignited a new hot shiver in her.

Her body was alive and on fire, causing her to writhe and thrash on the bed.

She sucked in a breath as Sawyer's fingers and lips touched her swollen, wet folds. Every part of her shook as he lifted her legs over his shoulders and dove down on her pussy with his greedy mouth. The heat that he sent into her slickened flesh from his trailing tongue was unimaginable and shocking. Never had she felt these kinds of sensations. When Sawyer applied pressure to her clit with his tongue, explosive jolts suddenly rocked her entire body.

Nicole grabbed a fistful of his hair trying to steady herself, but it didn't work. Nothing was steady. Nothing was calm. Quite the opposite. Even the room seemed to be spinning, burning, thundering like her body.

"God. It's so…"

Reed swallowed her words with his mouth, kissing her until she thought she might actually pass out. He released her lips. "How delicious is Chicago?" he asked Sawyer.

"Sweet cream, bro. The sweetest I've ever tasted in my life."

"I thought so." Reed's hot wicked eyes peeled away her defensive layers with ease. "I can't wait to feel your tight pussy around my cock, sweetheart. What do you think about that?"

She groaned, unable to answer as Sawyer once again buried his face between her thighs. His lusty licks drove her mad with shaky desire. She could no longer hold back her screams.

"Music to my ears, Chicago." Reed's lips feathered her nipples.

"Let us hear your cries of pleasure."

Sawyer's groans reverberated over her clit, making her even wetter. "So fucking good. God, I could sample you all night. Come for us, baby. Drown me with your cream."

"I–I can't…I never…never been able to…"

"Shhh." Reed's hand covered her mouth. "You will come tonight, Nicole. Trust me. And more than once, I promise."

She wanted to believe him, already feeling more sensations inside her body than ever before. "But what if I can't?"

Before she could give them the million reasons why she couldn't, Sawyer began nibbling on her clit and thrusting his fingers into her pussy, hitting a spot that erupted into immense pulsating sensations that flooded her body. There was no doubt about what this was, her first climax ever. She'd never dreamed it would be so piercing and consuming. Her body was in charge, not her mind. Her pussy clenched and unclenched and clenched again. She could feel the liquid pouring out of her and into Sawyer's ready mouth. And still she came and came and came.

She could hear herself scream but it sounded far away and distant to her, as the quakes in her body seemed to scream even louder. Reed's and Sawyer's licks and kisses were giving her the most supreme pleasure she'd ever felt in her life. Hot heady waves rolled through her again and again. Over and over. Stronger and stronger.

Sawyer pushed his finger in deeper into her pussy and started sucking her clit into his mouth, causing a new round of shattering trembles to flood her body. Every muscle tightened, every cell fired, every breath came out a scream. The incredible intensity went on and on until she was totally limp.

Sawyer moved up her body, returning to the place on her side he'd been earlier. He brushed his lips on her shoulder. Reed nibbled on her neck. Her heart pounded in her chest as she trembled between them.

"How do you feel, Chicago?" Reed asked, continuing to trace his fingertips over her body.

"It's hard to describe, but I feel great." She looked up at the faces staring down at her. God, they were gorgeous men. "Really great."

"Just wait until we get inside your gorgeous body." Reed's sweet lascivious grin let her know he wasn't even close to being done with her tonight.

Sawyer smiled broadly. "Your pleasure pleases us, baby, more than you can know."

Still reeling from her orgasm, she was surprised at how her pussy seemed to react to their lusty talk as it throbbed and ached once again. This wasn't her norm. For chrissakes, she was a cop—maybe benched at the moment, but still a gun-toting, badge-wearing Chicago police officer. So why was she acting like a frail, fainting woman? Because these two cowboys seemed to know every spot on her body that could work her into a stupor, and God what a stupor.

"You're so beautiful, Chicago." Reed ran his hand up her neck.

She bit her bottom lip to keep from pleading with them for more. Trying to raise her mental walls back up but failing miserably, she closed her eyes tight.

"Don't, Chicago." Reed's voice was filled with sharp warning.

When she felt his fingers on her chin, she opened her eyes. "Don't what?"

"You know what I mean. Don't pull back. Keep yourself open." His tone softened. "I want you to experience more pleasure than you've ever had before. I want tonight be unforgettable for you."

"It already is," she confessed, feeling the sting of grateful tears in her eyes. "I want you to enjoy tonight as much as I do. Fair is fair. I'm a modern woman." She reached between both their legs and grabbed their big, hard dicks, one in each of her hands.

The lusty growls that came out of both of them thrilled her.

Sawyer's hot gaze seared into her. "Don't think you're in charge here, baby. You're not." His deep voice held more promise than threat and that delighted her.

"Isn't sex a fifty-fifty thing, or in this case three-thirds?"

"No," Reed said, wrapping his hand over hers, helping her stroke his cock. "It's a one hundred and ten percent thing and it's all for you, Chicago. Our pleasure comes from yours, understand?"

"Not really." Actually, not one bit, but God, she loved how focused they seemed to be on her. They took lovemaking to a new level, a level she'd never known was even possible.

"Fuck, I love your tits," Reed said, cupping them with his big hands.

Female police officers learned the ins and outs of male conversation from their very first day on the force. She was no exception. Even though she'd heard the word "tits" a million times back at the station, she'd never been fond of it. But the way Reed talked about her breasts, using that word didn't sound denigrating at all. He was clearly mesmerized by her chest, hell, her entire body, and that added to her own excitement.

"You want more, Nicole?" Sawyer's thick fingers threaded through her ripe pussy, but he seemed to make sure he never touched her clitoris. The teasing was driving her mad.

"Yes. God, yes."

Suddenly, Reed fisted himself. She gazed at his cock as the head began to weep a drop of pre-cum. "Let's condom up."

She heard the sound of a wrapper tearing behind her. She turned and saw Sawyer rolling a condom down his dick. Another rip, pulled her attention back to Reed, who was sheathing his cock with a rubber, too.

I'm doing this? I'm actually going to do this? Her logic tried to claw its way back to the front of her brain, but it couldn't seem to get through the flood of need inside her. She wasn't about to stop them. Never had she wanted something so much as she wanted them to be inside her, to fill her, to merge her body with theirs in the most intimate of ways.

"I want your pussy, Chicago. I will have your pussy tonight."

He rolled on top of her and she could feel his cock on her slick folds and even on her clit, which made her groan. Reed kissed her and then thrust into her pussy. The advance of his massive cock into her body made her groan.

"Nice and tight. Damn, baby. I love it." He plunged in and out of her, stretching her channel wider and wider with every inch he claimed. "How long, Chicago?"

"Too long," she confessed. "Way too long, and no one as big as you."

His smile thrilled her. "Like I said, you won't forget this night. I promise you that." Then he thrust back in deeper, shifting his hips, adding to the already overwhelming pressure building inside her. She gazed into his blue eyes and saw such beauty, such perfection. His strokes came hard and fast into her pussy, over and over. The sweet friction she was feeling ripped through her, especially in a place inside her channel that she now believed must be her G-spot as it ignited powerful quakes that started there and spread out through the rest of her body.

Without a word, Reed pulled his cock out of her and she immediately missed him being inside her. Shocked and thankful, she realized what these brothers meant to do. Reed slid off her body and was replaced by Sawyer. His hooded gaze mesmerized her as he crashed his lips into her. His kiss was urgent and hot, and he didn't wait to shove his massive cock into her wet pussy. She could feel his hands on her hips as he began pumping into her like a mad man. He leaned back, continuing to thrust into her body. The passion she saw on his face enflamed her even more and the pressure inside her continued to build and multiply.

Reed tore off the condom and placed the head of his cock on her throbbing lips. "Suck me, Chicago. Swallow all of me."

Lost in the hot haze of their lovemaking, she licked the tip of his dick, drinking down the tiny pearl of pre-cum. It tasted salty and spicy.

"Fuck, yeah." He groaned as she parted her lips and slid down his shaft.

As Sawyer plunged deeper and deeper into her greedy pussy, she sucked on Reed's cock until her cheeks hollowed out.

Suddenly, her flesh ignited and pulsed as her next orgasm exploded inside her. Sawyer continued to thrust into her, and then she felt his body stiffen in one final deep shove of his cock into her pussy. The sound that came out of him was part groan and part growl, an intense note of release.

Reed plunged his dick into her mouth until she felt his hot liquid hit the back of her throat. "Fuck."

She swallowed as much of his cock as she could and drank down every drop of his seed. As her own climax continued to ripple through her entire body, Reed and Sawyer moved back to their former positions on the bed, sandwiching her between their big, muscular bodies.

"Thank you, Chicago." Reed nuzzled her neck.

"I should be thanking you two," she said.

Sawyer stroked her hair, helping her ride out the rest of her climax. "Wait until morning, baby."

She turned her head to him. "Why?"

"The night's not over yet." He planted his lips on hers, capturing her mouth completely. His tongue swept in and she opened herself to the hungry intrusion.

Reed nibbled on her breasts, and she felt the pressure once again begin to build inside her. She knew her heart was in danger with these two, but she couldn't stop herself from diving over the edge into their promises of more of tonight's pleasure. Tomorrow, she would face reality. Tonight, she wanted to get lost in the dream and in their arms.

Chapter Nine

As the morning sun peeked through the window, Sawyer leaned up on his elbow. Nicole slumbered between him and Reed, who was also sleeping. God, her slightly slack mouth and soft breathing was a sight to behold. She was beautiful. His night with her had been incredible. He'd been riveted by her the moment he'd met her. Once he and Reed got her up here to the cabin, he'd been completely enthralled. The talk he and Reed had had about her before the infamous moth incident had been enlightening. Reed could deny it all day long but he was into her, too.

Once they'd brought her to bed, made love to her, and watched her fall asleep in their arms, Sawyer knew he could never live without Nicole. How in the world would he be able to persuade her to stay in Destiny with him and Reed? And how could he convince his brother to let go of his fear of love and open himself up to the one woman that could change everything for them? Never had he faced a more daunting task and never had he wanted to succeed more. At stake were his happiness, his future, and his very heart.

Her long lashes fluttered open as she shook off sleep. She looked at him with her big brown eyes and started to speak.

He placed his index finger on her lush lips. "Shh." Then he pointed to Reed who was completely sacked out. His brother could sleep through anything. Still, he wanted to talk to her alone, so he didn't want to risk this being the time a little hushed talk might wake Reed.

She nodded, and then tilted her head to the doorway. She mouthed "okay" and then scooted down to the foot of the bed, swinging her long, silky legs off the mattress.

Sadly, she grabbed up one of the discarded towels from last night and wrapped it around her body. He instantly hated not being able to see her resplendent nakedness.

He wanted her again, but knew that would have to wait. Nicole needed time to collect herself, to reflect on what had happened. By the look on her face, her mental walls that had vanished last night were back in place.

Sawyer pulled on his jeans, believing Nicole would be comfortable with him clothed, but he didn't put on his shirt, not wanting her to be too comfortable. Having her a little unsettled might be just what he needed to get her guard back down. He followed her out of the bedroom and quietly shut the bedroom door behind him.

Wrapped up in the towel, she was sitting on the sofa with her legs under her and her arms folded around her ample chest. "Hey, cowboy."

"You told us you weren't an early riser."

She shrugged. "Things change, I suppose. What about you? I thought you needed coffee before conversation.

"I guess you're right. Things do change."

"I see you like being half dressed as much as I do," Nicole said with a sarcastic grin. "Much better than putting on binding clothes I suppose."

"If you want, I can go get your suitcase out of the bedroom."

She shook her head. "Let your brother sleep. I'll dress when he gets up."

He stared at Nicole. His heart started to thud in his chest and his cock began to swell. *Not now.*

"I recall you saying you're also a coffee drinker, right?" he asked.

She nodded. "Love it. I bet you two cowboys down several pots a day of the stuff."

"Nope. Two cups. No more." He took a seat on the sofa next to her.

She shifted closer to him so that her entire body was facing his direction. "Reed, too?"

"Two cups doctored up with cream and sugar. He even likes the foofoo java drinks. Whenever we're at a livestock auction in a big city he sneaks off at least once to get his fill of fancy coffees. Don't tell him I told you that."

She smiled. "He'd hate for me to know that about him, wouldn't he?"

"That's so true." This small talk was skirting the issue of what was really on his mind and likely hers, too. Nicole was in danger. "Tell me about the case you and Jason are working on."

Her lips tightened and she shook her head. "Too much to tell."

This was the wrong track with Nicole. She was defensive and guarded again. Why? Her past. If he was going to learn why she was on the Russian mafia's radar, he had to approach gingerly. "How long have you been on the force in Chicago?"

"Four years," she said with a sigh.

"Why police work?" His gut tightened at the thought of anyone hurting her. What was it that Jason had learned from her friend Henry that had derailed this strong and self-reliant woman to agree to come with him and Reed?

"I come from a long line of police officers. My grandfather was one of the most decorated members in the entire department." The pride in her voice told him she was opening up to him if only a little.

"He must be proud of you."

"*Was* proud of me. He passed away."

His own grief shot to the center of his chest, constricting his heart for a painful moment. "I'm sorry to hear that. How long?"

"Two years." She looked at him with a hard stare. "What about you? Family?"

Nicole was smart. She clearly wasn't comfortable with his probing so was trying to turn the tables on him. *Good move, but I'm a Dom, sweetheart. I've got moves you can't even imagine.* Once she was more susceptible to him, he would flip the switch and delve deeper into her secrets. For now, he decided to give her a little slack, knowing it would work to his advantage. Besides, he wanted to open up to her as much as he wanted her to open up to him.

"Just Reed and Erica. Our parents died September twenty-eighth in two thousand one in a plane crash." He closed his eyes, recalling the tragic day.

He felt her fingertips on his forearm. "Oh my God. I'm so sorry I brought this up."

He opened his eyes and looked at the most beautiful creature he'd ever seen in his entire life. Her eyes were brimming with tears of empathy for him.

"It was a long time ago. I'm okay now."

She wrapped her hand over his wrists and squeezed. "No one is ever really okay after losing a parent, especially not like you and your brother and sister did. You go to bed in one kind of world one day and wake up to a completely different one the next."

"That's so true." The connection he felt with her was growing with every syllable she spoke.

She sighed and leaned back. "You may have healed from your loss, Sawyer, but you were changed forever by it, too. The missing never really goes away, does it?"

He shook his head, feeling his heart swell in his chest. His whole life he'd known how to read people. It was a gift and a curse at times. But as much time as he'd spent with Nicole since yesterday, it was only now he was seeing her—really seeing her—for the first time. She had a depth of compassion that was remarkable to him. She was a survivor, too. Whatever crushing hurt had happened to her, she'd fought her way through it. Hell, it was clear she was still fighting the demons of her past. What were they?

"Tell me about your parents. What were they like?"

"Mom was the most selfless person I've ever known. Whenever she saw someone who needed help, she was there ready to lend a hand. Our two dads were so in love with her."

"Two dads? That's unusual."

"Not here in Destiny. It's quite common. Actually, it's the norm. Our dads were opposite on so many levels," Sawyer continued. "Reed is a lot like Dad Gene."

"A smart-ass," she said, smiling.

"I mean quiet, hard for him to open up."

"Yeah. I can feel that in him," she said. "What about your other dad? How are you like him?"

"Dad Gilbert was always accused of being able to read minds."

Her cheeks flared red. "And you have that ability, too?"

"Some say I do."

"What am I thinking right now then?"

He closed his eyes and made a humming sound to add to the show. "You are thinking how lucky you are to be with such a good-looking cowboy." He opened his eyes and laughed. "Right?"

Her jaw dropped and then snapped shut. "You should take your act on the road."

"And leave all this?" He motioned to the cabin. "Not a chance." Time to test the waters and see if he could turn this conversation around to learn more about her. "What about your loss, Nicole? Talk to me."

"I want to, cowboy." She released her hold on his wrists. "I just can't. You asked me about the case. What if I tell you about that first?"

It would have to do, for now. "Yes. I want to hear about it. You know we've had several killings in Destiny of late. One, just a couple of months ago at TBK."

"TBK?"

"Two Black Knights. It's a high-tech company owned by two local billionaires in Destiny."

Her jaw dropped. "Billionaires live in Destiny?"

"Actually, we have more than a few. Eric and Scott Knight are friends of ours. The Stone brothers—Emmett, Bryant, and Cody—aren't billionaires but aren't too far from it. I think Mrs. Steele is a billionaire, too, but I'm not sure. Gold, the owner of the club we met at, he's rumored to have over a million in cash under his mattress."

"Seriously?"

He nodded. "Then there are the O'Learys. They could buy and sell everyone in town, including all the other billionaires."

"That's an impressive demographic for any city but even more so for such a small town as Destiny."

He shrugged. "I suppose so. Growing up here, it seems quite normal to me."

He watched her eyes dart around the cabin. "You and your brother aren't part of that rich crowd, are you?"

"Nope. But they are friends. The Knights' and Stones' parents died in the same plane crash as ours. The entire town, but especially the O'Learys, were there for us."

"I'd like to meet your sister."

That was music to his ears. That had to mean Nicole might be convincible if not entirely open to staying yet. He felt light and hopeful. "You two will get along great." Taking a risk, he leaned forward and brushed the hair out of her eyes.

She rewarded him with a smile. "Phase Four seems out of place in such a small town, don't you think?"

Again, he shrugged. "Gold opened the club after his wife died years ago. He's got the money to keep it going, but nearly every citizen in town is a member. Besides, there's a big list of celebs that don't live here but come at least once or twice a year.

"No kidding."

"One thing about Destiny, we believe in discretion. The BDSM-Poly community is tight. The world may see our ways as fringe and eccentric, but we see it as the only way to live and love."

The door opened and out came Reed, yawning. He'd also put on jeans like Sawyer, but nothing else. "I'm starving. What do we have to eat?"

"Good morning to you, too, cowboy," Nicole said, shaking her head.

"Hey, beautiful. How are you this morning?"

Sawyer turned to their gorgeous guest. Her face was flushed. One thing about Reed, he always knew just what to say to get the response he wanted.

"I'm hungry, too, actually. What do you have?"

"Unfortunately, we only have beans and bread." Sawyer felt his own stomach rumble. "We were supposed to get groceries yesterday but got sidetracked."

Reed stepped up to Nicole and cupped her chin. "I'd starve any time to be sidetracked by you, Chicago."

Nicole raised one eyebrow. "You sure do have the lines, cowboy. Lots of them. Don't forget, I'm a cop. I know when someone is holding back."

Reed frowned but kept his hand on her chin. He didn't say a word for a bit. Reed was clearly trying to wrestle with his feelings for her. "Maybe we should get dressed and head to town to eat. We've got a diner, a Chinese restaurant, and a burger shop. What would you like?"

"I love Chinese."

"Deal."

An idea came into Sawyer's mind. These two needed time alone. "I think it would be better for me to get takeout. Jason wanted us to keep her here for two days, right?"

"True," Reed said.

She sighed. "I swear this area is fifty years behind the times. I suppose men here still like their women barefoot in the kitchen and pregnant, right?"

The image materialized in his head of her in just that condition, carrying their baby. He knew answering her would not win him any points. "What dish would you like from Phong's, Nicole?" he asked instead.

Chapter Ten

Nicole sat in a chair opposite Reed. The chairs were on the porch that she'd taken a bath on shortly after her arrival here. Had that only been yesterday? God, it seemed like a lifetime ago.

She looked up into the pale blue sky and thought there couldn't be a more beautiful place on the planet than right here.

Sawyer had been gone only ten minutes to head to town to get them Chinese food. Her mouth watered thinking about the sesame chicken he would bring back.

"What do you think of our Blue Arrow Peak?" Reed asked, pointing to the tallest snowcapped mountain off in the horizon.

She looked over at the cowboy, who was still wearing nothing but his jeans. She, on the other hand, had decided to dress. After, Reed had suggested they come out here to enjoy the morning. The idea had suited her fine.

"It's amazing. How long does the snow stay up there?"

"Year round. Most of the other tops melt off, but not Blue Arrow." His eyes seemed to sparkle with pride. Reed clearly loved where he lived, and she could understand why since the area was breathtaking. "Not the highest or biggest in the Rockies, but she's one in a million to me."

"The open air is something I don't get back home," she confessed. "It's quite nice." But it felt like more than that to her in truth. There was a peacefulness here that got into Nicole's bones and warmed every part of her. How long had she felt like the walls had been closing in on her? Years. Nicole sighed, feeling more relaxed than she had in ages and ages. "You know I can't stay here much longer, no matter what your sheriff says."

Reed brushed the hair out of her eyes. She was growing accustomed to his tender touch. "Tell me more about this investigation, Chicago. It's got a hold on you in ways you haven't told us yet, doesn't it?"

She shrugged, trying her best to put her poker face back on but having a difficult time of it. "It's something I want to do. Police work is my life."

"You seem to be a twenty-four-seven cop. Why so serious all the time? Do you ever do anything fun, Nicole?"

Nicole, not Chicago, this time? God, why couldn't she seem to keep her head straight around Reed or his brother? And when both were present? *Forget about it.* "Tell me about your sister," she said, hoping the change in subject would keep the topic off of her.

Reed smiled and took her hand and squeezed. "Sawyer told you about Erica?"

She nodded. "Is she like you or him?"

"A bit of both, but she's more like our mom actually." His face darkened but he didn't release his hold of her hand.

Reed evidently carried a lot of grief still, even though it had been quite a while since the tragedy. Sawyer had told her about losing their parents in a plane crash. She shouldn't have brought up family to Reed. *Always putting your foot in your mouth, Nicole, aren't you?* "Sorry, cowboy. My badge isn't on. It's off. Tell me about the club in Destiny. You guys are members?"

"We are." The tight lines that had appeared on his face a moment ago softened. "What do you know about BDSM, Chicago? You've got more than a couple of clubs there that cater to the life, right?"

"I know very little, though I have heard of the clubs you're talking about. Quite racy."

"Do you want to know about the life?" His question seemed to hold a challenge.

What was the correct answer he wanted from her? She wasn't

sure, but felt like there were more wrong ones than right. "I do. Please, fill me in. I want to know more."

He released her hand and leaned back in the chair, looking out at the vista in front of them. "'Want' is a powerful word, sweetheart. I want a lot of things, too, but I've learned that most of those will never be."

"That sounds so sad, Reed. I didn't take you for a pessimist."

"Realist." The hard edge in his tone flattened her.

She wished Sawyer were here now. He had the intuition she lacked. He would know how to handle Reed to get him back to the playful, mischievous cowboy she'd known of him so far. But Sawyer wasn't here. Reed was. She felt empathy for him. On the outside, she'd chosen to be closed off by retreating from the world to block her pain. Reed had clearly built his walls differently. His were made of lightheartedness, playfulness, and wicked flirtation. Not a retreat at all but a full-on frontal assault which worked the same to keep people from the real truth—that he carried his suffering every second of every day like her. He seemed open, but he was obviously as closed as she was.

"I'm sorry, Reed. Let's talk about something else. BDSM and the plane crash can be off-limits, okay?"

"No. They're on the table. What do you want to know about the plane crash?" His lips thinned into a sharp line.

"I can't even imagine what you went through when that happened." Her heart was breaking seeing the pain on his face. "I shouldn't have brought it up. Sawyer told me a little, but that's his version to tell. I don't need to know anything. I swear. Tell me about the mountain lion or anything else you want to talk about. Or we don't have to talk at all. Let's just wait until Sawyer gets back. Okay?"

He touched her cheek. "Shh, Chicago. It's okay. Erica and Sawyer have told me I should talk about it more, but I've never had a reason to—"

"That's why I shouldn't have brought it up, Reed." Tears of understanding brimmed in her eyes. Talking about his loss reminded her of her own and of her grandfather. She knew what it meant to lose someone you loved, someone you counted on, someone you failed. She hadn't been able to talk to anyone about her pain either. Though she admired his courage to delve so deep, this was getting too close to her own dark grief. She shouldn't push this. "Change of subject is in order."

He frowned. "You interrupted me, sweetheart, before I finished my sentence."

"I'm sorry, Reed."

"You keep saying that. Stop. Okay?"

She nodded.

"Damn, you're something else, Chicago. Destiny isn't quite ready for you I'm betting." His lips curled into a slight smile, but the pain on his face remained. "What I was going to say was I've never had a reason to talk about my parents' accident until you showed up."

She felt her eyes widen in surprise. "What do you mean? I'm not anyone special."

"You calling me a liar?"

"God, no."

"Then don't doubt me when I say this is the first time I've ever wanted to talk about this with anyone. You're special"

"I won't, but I'm not sure about how you see me." She'd ventured into this and wasn't going to back out now.

"That's better." He took in a deep breath and closed his eyes. "I was fifteen when it happened. Not really a boy anymore but not quite a man either. Mom was so excited that the Stones and Knights had included them on the vacation trip to Barbados. So were our dads. They were ranch hands, like Sawyer and me. They lived a simple life but a loving life. The Stones and Knights had always treated them as equals, though that was clearly not the case monetarily speaking. I suppose it had, as it does now, something to do with how Destiny ticks. We're quirky but loyal folk."

"I've seen that already about your town. Sheriff Wolfe is quite loyal in fact."

He opened his eyes and began stroking her hair. "Too ethical, also, if you ask me, but that's another story for another day. There's so much more to see and to know, Chicago. Destiny is simple but also complicated, easygoing but quick to blows, conservative about some things but quite liberal about others. We argue with each other like cats and dogs sometimes. You should see us around election time. Sweet little old ladies have been known to pull out their pistols and fire warning shots into the air over an ongoing issue about renaming Destiny's park."

She grinned. "Not quite Norman Rockwall is it."

"Not even close, but it's home. Always will be for me. My dads grew up here, too."

"So you're third generation. Do you call yourselves Destonites or Destiners?"

"Destonians is what most say," he informed.

"Has a nice ring to it. Are your grandparents still here?"

"No. They died before I was born. The O'Learys are like grandparents to us and to the others. Did Sawyer tell you about the other orphans?"

"He did. You all are close, right?"

"Like brothers."

"And I guess the Knights and Stones think of Erica as a sister, too."

"They do. She complains about having seven big brothers but I think she actually likes it. What about you, Chicago? Brothers or sisters?"

"Just me." Nicole felt her tension return as her dark past clawed at the back of her mind. "Fifteen is young to lose parents, Reed. Really young." She could relate. She'd never known her father. Her mother had vanished after dropping her off at school when she was only eight.

"I survived, sweetheart. That's what you have to do."

"I know, but it doesn't always make it any easier, does it?"

He sighed. "No. The world changed that day I lost my parents."

"It was in September, right?"

"Yes. The twenty-eighth, seventeen days after the attack on the World Trade Center in New York and the Pentagon in Washington on nine-eleven."

"I hadn't thought about that."

"Mom had. She was worried. You know they grounded all civilian aircraft until the thirteenth. I wish they'd done it for longer." His grief seemed to fill the air. "Dad Gene was the pilot. Did Sawyer tell you that?"

"No."

"Dad had several thousand hours in the air. He was in the Air Force and had flown fighter jets. Dad Gilbert had his license, too. Since he'd been in the Army on the ground, not as many hours in his logbook as Dad Gene, but still a few hundred. The plane was brand new. The weather was ideal."

"What happened to cause the crash?"

"The FAA ruled it pilot error, but none of us believe that." He stood up and Nicole saw that his hands were balled up into big fists. "Shit happens, Chicago. That's life."

She left her chair and came up to the giant cowboy and hugged him. "It shouldn't be that way, Reed." She felt her tears stream down her cheeks as his pain, his suffering, his loss filled her mind and mingled with her own sadness. "I've always had to be the responsible one, the self-reliant one no matter what the challenge."

She felt his arms come around her and pull her in tight.

"Me, too," he said in a tone softer and more serious than she'd ever heard from him.

She had to tell him. The words had to come out. "Maybe life has been harder for us because we hold everything in. I know it was the reason for my downfall." She closed her eyes and let the memories out that she'd shoved deep down. As ugly as her sins were, she wanted him to know all of it. She looked up into the blue eyes of the man that had once been a boy forced to grow up too fast. "You know I'm a cop. My whole family has deep roots in the department, several generations of police officers. What you don't know is my mother broke my grandparents' hearts. She was a drug addict. Heroin. My grandmother had a stroke and died after learning the truth about her daughter, my mother. My grandfather was too tough, but it changed him. The pride of Chicago's men in uniform, he never said it but I always knew he felt like a failure for my mother."

"Her shortfalls aren't yours, baby." He squeezed her a little tighter into him.

"I know. I have plenty of my own. My mother abandoned me when I was in the second grade. Eight years old. My grandfather took me in and became a single parent at the ripe old age of fifty-nine. God, he was so thrilled when I joined the force. It seemed to erase his guilt some."

"I can only imagine how happy you must've made him," he said, his voice low.

"Then? Yes. Later? No. I became his second disappointment. Shortly into my service he was diagnosed with Alzheimer's disease. It took his mind fast. I wasn't quite a rookie but I was still new to the force. I had to start caring for him and keep pulling my shifts. The pressure got to me. I couldn't sleep after he started calling me by my mother's name—Helen. It wasn't long before he started shouting at me as if I were her, his biggest failure." Nicole closed her eyes and sobbed. "I was so angry at him. I knew in my head that it was the illness, but I couldn't get my heart around the fact that he could confuse me for my mother."

"Chicago, that's normal. Anyone would have felt that way. You're too hard on yourself, sweetheart."

"Am I?" She averted her eyes, unable to look directly at him. "I couldn't sleep. I was going to work, coming home, trying to take care of him. I'd put my head on the pillow and my mind would spin and spin. Granddad had pain pills, prescription pain pills in his medicine cabinet. They were for his hip-replacement surgery that had occurred six months before his diagnosis of Alzheimer's. I started taking them at night just to get some rest. One a night became two and three and on and on. As they say 'the apple doesn't fall far from the tree' and I fell into the same mire my drug-addict mother fell into."

He cupped her chin. "Look at me, baby."

She couldn't resist and raised her gaze to meet his.

"You are not your mother, Nicole."

"You barely know me. How can you be sure?"

"Trust me, I know. You would never abandon anyone let alone a child like you were. Your mother did that, didn't she?"

She nodded, feeling her lower lip begin to quiver. "I'm still an addict, Reed. After my grandfather's death, I spiraled out of control. I thought I was only taking two or three pills a night to sleep but I was taking so much more." The day of her near demise and biggest mistake had been a weight she'd carried for two years. Telling Reed seemed to be lifting it some. "I came to the station during a photo op one day for our Police Commander. You know what I did? I threw up on him while the cameras were running. Yep. I disgraced the Flowers name that day. I ran out without so much as an apology to the commander."

"Baby, I'm so sorry."

"Now I've got you saying it," she smiled weakly. "I barely have any memory of that day I was so high on drugs. Two a night? I was delusional. It had to be much more. Patti, the only other female at the station, was my daily coffee run buddy. She found me an hour later at my apartment sprawled out on my living room floor with a bag of Oxycontin."

"Was that the drug your grandfather was given for his surgery?"

"No. I have no idea where that bag of shit came from. Seriously, I was messed up. Jaris, my partner at the time, showed up right after Patti. I would've died if it hadn't been for them. I would've lost my badge, too. They've kept my secret ever since, but they made sure I got clean. Jaris still goes with me to my addicts anonymous group three times a week."

"Were you ever in love with him, Chicago?" His voice was steady and calm as he touched her on the cheek.

Her jaw dropped. "Jaris?"

God, he was a lot of things to her but never boyfriend material. Sure, he was good looking, but he was more brother than anything.

"Help me understand what he was to you, Nicole."

"No. We were partners. We are friends. That's all. Nothing else."

He let out a long, heavy breath. "Good."

She wondered why he cared. Was he less of a player than she'd first imagined him to be?

"So this has something to do with why you're in Destiny?" Reed asked. "This case is connected in some way?"

"Nope. Patti and Jaris are the only people who know what really happened that day. The rest of the station believes I was suffering from the flu. It still landed me behind a desk for the past two years, but I have my badge."

"That seems harsh to me."

She shrugged. "Maybe. The station commander isn't fond of me at all. He would love to see me off the force or at least out of his station."

"Asshole."

"Most definitely."

"So why didn't you leave the force?" he asked.

"I don't know. Family history, I suppose."

"Chicago, you were doing so good." He stepped back, releasing his hold of her. She instantly missed his embrace. "I'm disappointed in you."

She'd let him down in some way. "What do you mean?" she

asked, feeling the sting.

The playful Reed was gone. Here, in front of her, was the serious Reed, the demanding Reed, the dangerous Reed. If not careful, she would lose her heart to him even though he would most certainly crush it. Where was Sawyer? God, she needed him to run interference for her. He'd shown another side to him when they'd made love, but at his core she knew Sawyer would do his best to make sure she was okay. Reed wasn't afraid to push her, to test her limits, and that was something she was anxious about.

His eyebrows shot up. "You're lying to me about why you've stayed in a station where you believe you only have two friends who give a damn about you and the rest would rather see you go. Right?"

"It's a very long and complicated story, Reed." She dropped her gaze to the floor, but he cradled her chin in his big hand, gently urging her to look up. She did and saw his unblinking stare, which reached into her and squeezed more than his hug had earlier.

"Tell me why you stayed. Be honest."

"I can't fail my grandfather. I can't. It's not right. I will do what I have to do. You said it yourself. Shit happens. That's life."

"True, and you said that it shouldn't be that way, and I'm beginning to believe you might be right. Someone as amazing and courageous as you shouldn't have to face such things alone."

"Maybe not, but I have. I will continue to get through whatever the day brings me. You see why I get you, cowboy?"

"You think you get me, Chicago?" He tilted his head to one side.

She nodded. "You're angry. You're sad. You're so sad. You feel an aching emptiness in your very gut and still you go on. You do what you have to do. So do I. I told myself a million times it would be better to leave the force and go get another job, but I can't. Hell, I won't. I'm not someone who waves the white flag. Neither are you, right? You've been shrinking away from life with a wicked laugh and lusty grin hoping no one will see past your mask. I'm not someone who gets people normally, but I get you. I recognize the pain in you.

Mine is different but the impact is the same. Is that why you go to the club? Is that why you run to that kind of life? So you can remain alone and cut off from everyone even in a crowd?"

"No," he said, his fingers sinking into her hair. "BDSM is about control, Chicago. I need it to the very depths of my being. It makes sense of the world to me."

"And it protects you from opening up to others, too. Right?"

"Quiet," he snapped, tugging on her hair. "You want to know about the life, then listen good. There are loving relationships that are formed and solidified in the lifestyle that Sawyer and I practice. Long term, unbreakable relationships. BDSM is about trust, plain and simple. The more a sub trusts her masters the more pleasure she enjoys and the more satisfaction her Doms get."

"I get that, Reed. My question is so what is holding you back from choosing a sub for you and Sawyer? Sawyer seems ready to settle down. You don't. Am I wrong?"

He released her hair. "Doesn't matter if it's me or Sawyer or both. It is what it is."

"The hell it doesn't. What are you afraid of, cowboy?"

He jerked her back into his body. "I'm not afraid of anything."

"Really? Now who is lying?"

"Tell me this, Nicole. How long are you in Destiny for?"

"You know that already. A week or so."

He kissed her, pressing his lips to her mouth. She kept her eyes open, watching his go hazy with desire. Her own passion was heating up to a roaring blaze. She felt her toes curl and a tingle spread from the center of her abdomen and out through the rest of her body.

Suddenly, Reed ended their kiss. "Run back to your desk, Chicago. That's where you belong. I belong here. You worry about your life and I'll worry about mine. It's the way it's got to be." And then he walked into the cabin, leaving her alone with the half breaths he'd created in her with his kiss.

Chapter Eleven

Reed stared at Nicole as she walked into the cabin with swollen red eyes. God, he hated himself right now more than he ever had before. How the hell was he going to fix things with her? He couldn't.

"Sawyer should be back any minute," Reed told Nicole—the one woman he couldn't stop thinking about.

"Fine." She sat down on the opposite side of the sofa, her cop act back in place. It was obviously what she put on to protect herself from assholes like him.

He knew he had frozen up when she'd gotten too close to his truth. *Close? She'd nearly hit the nail on the head.* He could've handled things better. She deserved at least that much from him. What could he say to fix things, to help her understand why he acted the way he did? Words were his strong suit when it came to seducing a cute sub to bed, but a woman like Nicole was due the truth. Those words, candid and honest words, never came easy for him. He'd lived his whole life keeping things casual and laid-back. Nicole was kind, warm, a woman who wasn't afraid to stand up and fight. God, she was everything he needed and more. He wanted to tell her that, with all his heart, but what would that change? Nothing. She would go back to Chicago, to her life there. He would stay here with Sawyer, who was in as deep as he was—wanting a future with her.

"When your brother gets back, I'm going to have him take me back to town, Reed. I'm done here."

Fuck! "We'll see about that." He was pushing her away. If not now, when was the right time to tell her how much she meant to him?

"I'm a free woman, cowboy. I can come and go as I please. Trust me on that one." She patted the side of her jacket where he knew her gun was hidden underneath.

"You mean to shoot me then, Chicago?" That would be better than to live a single day knowing he'd never confessed his true feelings to her. Feelings? They always got a person in trouble and he was no exception.

Before she could answer, Sawyer walked in through the front door carrying the takeout from Phong's. The aromas of their various dishes wafted through the air, causing Reed's stomach to growl.

"Breakfast is served," Sawyer said, placing the sacks on the table.

Nicole's dark mood seemed to fade the moment he'd walked in the door. "Thank God. I am starving."

Reed was, too, but his mind was on other things than his gut. Sawyer, too, was downright sunny around her. The way he looked at her, the way he acted around her, it was quite clear he was completely falling for her, head over heels, in way deep and going deeper.

"Here's the lady's sesame chicken." Sawyer handed Nicole her entrée that was in a familiar Phong's little white box. Hiro Phong had switched the restaurant's old plain container to the current one seven years ago. On the top was printed Phong's address and phone number. On the bottom, it was blank. The sides held the big change that had occurred back during Dragon week that year. Each side had an image of one of the four dragons of Central Park. Patrick O'Leary had been thrilled with the change. "Here's your kung pao beef, Reed."

"Thanks."

"And for me, chicken chow mein. But I got two dishes for us to share. I think you'll love them, Nicole."

"What are they?"

With a little fanfare, much like a magician about to pull a rabbit out of his hat, Sawyer opened the last two boxes of food. "Spinach and pork wontons."

She leaned over, peering in the container. "They look and smell delicious."

"Wait until you taste them." Sawyer reached over and touched her on the shoulder. He'd never seen his brother this way around any other woman. "And last but definitely not least, crab rangoon."

"I've never had that before."

"You'll love them. They're bite-size, fried dumplings stuffed with crab. It's like heaven for your taste buds, sweetheart."

"Sounds divine."

Sawyer turned to him with one eyebrow raised. "What's up with you?"

Sometimes it would've been nice to have a brother who couldn't read him like an open book. "Not a damn thing, if you must know."

Sawyer frowned. "Liar. You're usually halfway done with your meal by now." His brother turned to Nicole. "Is everything okay here?"

Her dark mood clearly snapped back into place. "We're fine. Let's eat."

Sawyer didn't push it, thank God.

As they all three ate their meal in silence, Reed felt the battle inside him rage. He wasn't ready to talk about his feelings with his brother or anyone. His emotions were more intense than he'd ever known them to be. His steady, calm control had apparently vacated the premises.

Nicole was a dream, the perfect woman for them except for a couple of things. Sawyer might be able to live a life without BDSM being a part of it, but he couldn't. Sure, a vanilla tumble now and again was fun but it didn't speak to him the way having a sub surrender fully to him did. God, he would love seeing that kind of trust in Nicole's eyes, hearing it on her lips, touching it on her skin. But he'd been in the life since he became an adult. He knew the risks and the rewards. She didn't. He couldn't even imagine her agreeing to the type of relationship he needed. Reed could almost see his way clear of ditching the life for a future with Nicole but for the biggest thing that held him back. He was falling for her hard. It would be okay for Sawyer to be in love with her. In an odd way, Reed had always expected his brother to end up that way once they settled on a wife. But he couldn't be with a woman in a permanent relationship that he cared for beyond fondness.

No way. No how. Never.

But with every bite he swallowed and every glance he stole of Nicole during the meal, Reed felt his ancient vow, the one he'd made shortly after the plane crash, weaken. Still, he could recite the oath he'd written in his journal all those years ago by memory.

Love is destined to fail. It failed me. My parents are gone despite the love they felt for each other. I loved them and it didn't save them one bit. I will not be a fool and fall victim to it again. I love my brother and sister. That is enough. I will do whatever I can to ensure they stay safe. I will marry a woman with Sawyer, but I will not love her. This I vow until the day I die.

A grieving teen's way of coping with horrific loss at the time, but now a mantra he'd come to live by. But how could he continue holding fast to that pledge after meeting Nicole? God knew he needed to. Love wasn't ideal. Sure, it could change a person's thoughts, feelings, even actions—but it could also crush them into a pile of despair. When Love was good and firing on all cylinders, it felt ecstatic. When the object of someone's affection was taken away tragically or otherwise, the heartbreak that followed was devastating.

"You're deep in thought, Reed. That's not like you," Sawyer said, pulling him back to the here and now.

"Just enjoying Phong's best," he lied.

Sawyer shook his head.

"It is good," Nicole said, gazing at him with her big eyes, ripping his resolve to shreds. "Best I've ever had."

God, he wanted to believe that love existed, but how could he after so long of believing it wasn't for him, believing it was overrated? He'd become an island of sorts, pushing people away.

After finishing their meal, Sawyer produced three fortune cookies that Hiro had sent for them. "Shall we see what our future holds?"

Nicole smiled, breaking his heart even more. "My grandfather and I had a tradition back in Chicago to help the magic really work. Our favorite Chinese restaurant always gave us more cookies than we needed, four or five each. Granddad would choose one from the lot to be my true fortune and I would choose his." The tone in her voice seemed to be the result of a mix of her sweet recollections about her grandfather and deep sadness for losing him.

That's what love gets you in the end. Heartache.

"Let's do that now," Sawyer said.

"What do you mean?" Nicole asked.

"You want me to pick a fortune cookie for you, bro?" he asked Sawyer.

"Yep. I'll pick one for Nicole and she'll pick one for you. We could use a little magic today."

"You don't have to do that for me, Sawyer." Nicole turned her gaze to Reed. "Unless you don't mind."

What was wrong with him? Wasn't a chance at real love staring him right in the face? The vow he'd taken after his parents' death was out of date and obsolete since Nicole's arrival. He wanted to stop running away from love. Could he? *Time to test the waters.* "I don't mind, Chicago. Let's do this tradition of you and your granddad's."

Her lips curled up into the cutest smile he'd ever seen in his life. She took the three cellophane-wrapped cookies from Sawyer and began studying them intently. She took her traditions seriously. Then Nicole selected one and handed it to Reed.

He took it, feeling the resolve to go for it, to give love a real try, to not hold back but to embrace what his emotions were screaming at him to do.

"Now you pick for Sawyer," she said.

He did, handing it to him.

"Thanks, bro," Sawyer said. "That leaves this one for you, Nicole." He gave her the last cookie.

"Now we read our fortunes. You'll see I was right about the magic."

"You first, Chicago. This is your tradition."

"You're right." She ripped off the clear wrapper and cracked the fortune cookie in half. In a flash, the cookie was devoured. "God, those are good."

"Homemade right here in Destiny." Sawyer nodded. "The fortunes are handwritten by Hiro's wife, Melissa."

"That's very impressive, cowboy." Nicole read hers first. "No one can walk backward into the future." That sounded like the fortune he needed, more scolding than prediction he thought. To him it meant he shouldn't let his past dictate his future.

"Now what?" he asked her.

"Sawyer's turn."

"You have a deal, sweetheart." Sawyer read his fortune. "Today, your mouth might be moving but no one is listening. That sounds about right."

"What do you mean by that, big brother? I listen."

"Like a stump," Sawyer said. "You read yours."

"We've got to feed the horses, or have you forgotten all your ranch duties? Playtime is over."

"I took care of that before I headed to town." Sawyer sighed. "Time for you to take center stage and be serious for a change. She needs us to be at our best."

"Macho much?" Nicole asked. "Guys, you have to know that I'm no shrinking violet. I am a strong woman who can take care of herself."

"I believe you, baby," Sawyer said, and then turned to him. "Read your fucking fortune now, before you piss me off."

"You've got a deal, Chicago." He cracked open his cookie, shoving both pieces into his mouth. He took the tiny slip that Melissa Phong had written on, shocked at the message on it.

"What does it say, cowboy?" she asked.

It was right then reading those words that he realized Nicole was for him and Sawyer. Love deserved a chance no matter the risk. BDSM or not, he would do whatever it took for her to agree to stay in Destiny and not return to Chicago.

He looked right into her brown eyes and saw his forever there.

Nicole chewed on her lower lip. "Well?"

He told her what was on his fortune and saw her eyes light up and her cheeks turn red. Ready to make a new and better vow, he glanced back at the prophetic words on the slip of paper.

Happiness is right in front of you.

Feeling the magic that Nicole's grandfather's tradition about the fortune cookies had invoked, Reed moved his eyes back to *her*—the woman he wanted as his own with everything inside him.

"Someone's coming," Sawyer said, pulling him from his thoughts.

Like his brother, Reed moved his fingertips to the gun in the holster, which was strapped to his side like always.

Nicole had her gun out and in her hand.

"You should head to the bedroom until we say you can come out," Sawyer said.

"Like I told you two before—I'm not helpless."

God, she needed a firm hand in the worst way. He prayed she would take to the life like he had. It was second nature to him now. Even if that long shot happened and she agreed to be trained by him and Sawyer, it would take many sessions to get her to trust them fully.

Sawyer walked to the window and peered out. His shoulders shifted downward, a silent motion that told Reed whoever was coming wasn't a threat to Nicole.

"Who is it?" she asked.

"It's Erica. Our sister," Sawyer informed.

Reed felt his shoulders sag. He was glad his sister had come to the cabin. She'd seemed sad and blue since that day at TBK. He missed the carefree, sunny Erica from before. He was sure that she and Nicole would get along, but even more, he hoped that Nicole, being a cop, would be able to help his sister understand she'd done nothing wrong.

What they all heard next made every muscle inside Reed tighten.

A gunshot.

Chapter Twelve

Nicole pulled out her gun and pointed it to the door. Whoever had fired the shot wasn't too far away by the sound of the gunfire.

Sawyer and Reed both had their guns drawn, too. Sawyer ran for the door, opened it, and pulled his sister inside. "Get down."

As he slammed it shut, Erica dropped to the floor.

"Over here," Nicole whispered in her best cop voice.

"I should've brought my gun," their sister said in a trembling tone.

Sawyer stared at Erica. "A gun?"

"Dylan has been training me to shoot. I want to know how to defend myself."

Nicole remembered meeting Dylan the day before in Sheriff Wolfe's office. He was a former federal agent, so he certainly would know his way around firearms. Erica had a good teacher.

"Good to know, little sister. Everyone should know how to take care of themselves." Sawyer ruffled his sister's hair.

Nicole called on her police training and considered the situation.

One shot. No more.

What had happened? Was it one of the Russians coming for her?

Sawyer cautiously peered back out the window.

"See anything?" Reed said quietly.

He shook his head.

Suddenly, they all heard a motorcycle engine rev up.

"You head out back to make sure there's not two of them. I'll go out front. Meet you at the truck," Sawyer said, running out the door.

"Nicole, you know what to do," Reed said as he headed out the back to the porch where she'd had her bath.

Even though her heart was slamming into her ribs, she kept her head. She did know what to do. Keep her gun ready at all times. Keep Erica calm. Keep herself calm. It was quite the task, but a necessary one.

"Hi Erica. I'm Nicole," she said in a steady voice that surprised even her. "I'm a cop. You're in good hands. And you know your brothers will be safe and have things under control in no time."

"I want to believe you, but I've been through this kind of thing recently. I'm definitely the one to blame for that incident, and maybe this one, too." Erica wiped tears from her eyes. "I know about you, Nicole. The whole town does. I came up here, knowing how my brothers live. Rustic. God. I brought you a care package that I thought you might need. Did those Russians follow me here? How stupid can I be?"

Nicole squeezed Erica. "No, this is all my fault. I brought all this to your town, not you."

The brothers' sister turned to her. "You understand what I'm going through, don't you?"

"As much as anyone carrying guilt can, Erica."

"Nicole, are you sure that Reed and Sawyer are going to be okay? I would die if anything ever happened to them."

So would I. "Yes. We just have to be calm. We've got to trust that they know what to do."

* * * *

Sawyer and Reed had given up the chase of the motorcycle. They'd never actually seen it, but only heard if from afar. Now, they couldn't even hear it. On foot, he and Reed—pistols still drawn— were headed to where they believed the motorcycle's engine had first turned over.

Reed pointed to the ground up ahead. "You see that?"

He nodded. "Looks like blood."

As they got closer, they saw a body on the ground that shocked Sawyer.

Connie. Their mountain lion was down. She'd been shot. Her breathing was labored.

"Be careful, Reed," he said as his brother knelt down beside the wild cat.

Reed nodded. "There's material in her paw, bro. Connie took some of the asshole's flesh."

"Doesn't surprise me one bit." Sawyer looked through the trees and saw the cabin's front door. Knowing how close the killer had come to succeeding in his mission sent a chill down his spine.

Reed took off his shirt.

"Careful. She might wake up," he cautioned his brother.

"I will, but we can't just let her die," Reed said. "You know what she just did, don't you? Erica could've died today."

Sawyer nodded, knowing that Connie had saved their sister's life. Whoever the motorcyclist was must've thought Erica was Nicole. "I'll go get the truck so we can get her to the cabin."

* * * *

Nicole looked at the magnificent animal in the bed of the guys' truck. She hated seeing Connie this way, eyes closed, jaw agape, breathing shallow. "We've got to get her to a vet."

"We can't leave. You know that. Whoever shot our girl got away, likely back to Destiny, crosshairs ready for any sign of you."

"You just can't let her die," Nicole said, feeling the sting of unshed tears in her eyes.

"Reed and I know a thing or two about taking care of big animals," Sawyer said gently. "We work on a ranch, you know?"

Erica nodded. "Nicole, they know what they're doing. Believe me. I've seen my brothers work miracles."

"Erica, take Nicole to the barn. Get all the towels you can find.

Fill up a bucket with water. Get the black case marked 'animal med supplies,'" Reed ordered. "It's next to the drench and the fly spray. Got it?"

"Yes," their sister answered.

"Good. Bring everything back here," he added. "Hurry. Sawyer and I will remove the bullet and will need those things pronto."

Nicole ran beside Erica to the barn, praying for Connie, the big cat she felt a deep connection to.

* * * *

Reed took a swig of the whiskey his brother had just brought him. It had been a very long night, but Connie had pulled through. She was heavily sedated and resting. He and Sawyer had modified her stall to ensure if she did wake she couldn't get out.

It would take a few days, maybe even a week, for her to get back on all four paws, but she was going to be okay. Thank God, the shot hadn't damaged any of Connie's internal organs, having entered her side. A fraction of an inch in any other direction would've taken the big cat's life for sure.

Luckily, all the livestock were still in the pasture and would remain there until Connie fully recovered.

"Look at those two," Sawyer said, pointing to Nicole and Erica, both asleep in the stall across from Connie's.

He shook his head and smiled. "How many times did we tell them to go into the cabin and rest?"

"At least two dozen, bro." Sawyer yawned. "They're both so stubborn."

"We owe Dylan for taking care of our sister." Reed took another swallow of the amber liquid.

Sawyer smiled. "Maybe he's finally ready to pull his head out of his ass and make a move on her. Cam's been ready for a while. It's just Dylan holding things up."

Reed looked at Nicole. *Time to pull my head out of my ass, too.* He was ready now. How did such a tender treasure like her find her way to Destiny, to Coleman Territory, to him and Sawyer? "I want her, Sawyer," he confessed. "Not just for a few nights or a long fling. I want her forever."

"So do I, Reed. So do I." Sawyer put his arm around his shoulder. "You've got to let Nicole know what you want. Right?"

He nodded, hoping for the perfect time to tell her.

* * * *

Nicole felt more connected than she had in her entire life. She was in a barn outside Destiny, Colorado, with Sawyer and Reed, the two cowboys Sheriff Jason Wolfe had forced on her, looking at a sleeping mountain lion.

Watching how skilled and gentle they'd been with Connie last night had reached deep into Nicole's heart, making it swell up with pride for them.

Erica was asleep inside the cabin. Sawyer and Reed had refused to let her return to Destiny alone until the shooter was found.

These cowboys had been strangers to her just a short time ago but now they were…what to her now? She really didn't know how to describe what she felt for them, but it was intense. Love? Maybe. If so, she'd have to move her debacle in the station two years ago down a notch. Foolishly, she'd actually opened up her heart to Sawyer and Reed. The new topper of her unwritten but often quoted too-stupid-to-live list would have to be that now.

Even though Sawyer seemed interested in something more lasting, Reed had made it quite clear on the porch the day before that he wasn't. Giving in to Sawyer's sweet advances might be wonderful and what she wanted deep down, but she couldn't. It would most definitely create a wedge between the two brothers, which she wasn't about to do. With all their brotherly sparring, it was so clear to her how much they loved one another. Sure, they'd grown up in an unusual home with two dads and one mom. Did that matter, really? Until the tragic plane crash, they'd been surrounded by love. Three parents had to be better than two. She'd not even had one parent to love her. Thank God for her grandfather. A poly family was what Sawyer and Reed were meant to have. One woman they could both cherish. She wasn't about to break up that dream for them even if that meant losing them both and ripping her heart in two.

They heard a vehicle coming up the road. They all pulled out their guns. Reed went to the barn door. "Relax. It's the sheriff."

He put away his gun. She heard the engine stop. "We're over here in the barn, Jason," Reed yelled.

The sheriff walked into the barn wearing the same kind of uniform he'd been wearing when she'd met him—a crisp, starched khaki shirt and pants. He tipped his hat to her. "Flowers."

"Sheriff," Nicole answered back. As much as she wanted to get to the bottom of the case and clear Henry's name, she couldn't help but feel heartbroken that her stay might be coming to an abrupt end. "Fill me in."

Reed moved next to her, creating an anxious, sad brew inside her. The sooner she was out of his hair, out of this cabin, out of Destiny, Colorado, the better. But she knew that wasn't completely true. Once she left for Chicago never to return, her heart wouldn't recover.

Sawyer walked over and stood by Sheriff Wolfe. She couldn't seem to be able to rein her mind in. Visions of her time with Sawyer and Reed swirled in her head. The trip up the mountain between the rugged cowboys had chipped away at her walls. When she'd spotted Connie, the graceful mountain lion in the middle of the dirt road, another chip fell away. Taking her bath on their porch snapped several more bits off her invisible barriers. The dream had demolished more. The moth, too, had been a part of the spell. And the most powerful elements of the magic had been Sawyer and Reed. Sexy. Charming. Funny. Kind. Too good to be true.

She'd fallen for them hard. Even after learning what kind of family they wanted, she'd let herself imagine what a life with them loving and sharing her would be like.

I'm a fool.

"I've got some troubling news, Nicole," the sheriff said. The caution in his tone shocked her. "Your friend Henry is missing. I tried to call him at the station, but they said he hadn't shown up for work."

"Maybe he's out sick." But she knew Henry better than that. He prided himself in his perfect attendance record at the station. He'd never missed a day of work in his entire career.

"I checked with the desk sergeant. He told me Henry hadn't bothered to call in. Does that sound like your friend, Flowers? I only talked with him a couple of times over the phone, but he didn't seem to be a man who would no-show anything."

Nicole immediately felt regret and dread sweep through her. She shouldn't have left Chicago, shouldn't have left Henry. "Any leads, Sheriff?"

"About Henry? No."

"I've got to get back to Chicago immediately."

"No way," Sawyer snapped. "You're staying here."

She wondered if the edge in his tone was more about keeping her in Destiny or keeping her safe. Maybe it was a little of both. "Sawyer, Henry is like family. I have to go find him. He probably is in trouble because of me."

"Trouble with a capital 'T' would be my guess, Chicago." Reed put his hand on her arm. "More the reason you have to stay with us."

"Just stop, cowboy." Her heart clanged in her chest, rocking her entire body. One minute Reed was flirty. The next he was pushing her away. Now, he was acting like he wanted her by his side so he could play bodyguard. "I'm sick of your macho BS. I'm a cop. I carry a gun. I've been trained. I know more than a little about how to protect myself." The words were coming out more sharp and angry than she wanted but still they came. Like water rushing through a broken dam, there was no stopping them. "I've been on my own a long time—long before I came to Destiny. Read my lips. I. Don't. Need. You."

Sawyer walked over and stood beside her, opposite Reed. "What the fuck happened while I was in town?" he asked Reed.

Reed didn't answer or even turn to him. Instead, his steely blue eyes fixed on her, making her shiver. She wasn't about to look away even though everything inside her was pushing her to do just that. He might've broken her heart, but he wouldn't win this stare off, a poor consolation, but the only one she could have.

After a lengthy silence, he finally spoke. "Chicago, I need you to trust me." Then he brushed the hair out of her eyes, and Nicole felt the sting of hopeful tears.

No. Don't fall down that rabbit hole again, Nicole.

"I want to, Reed. I really do, but you of all people have to understand why I can't."

"Can't or won't?" he asked.

"A little of both. Henry is in trouble. I'm not like Sawyer with his sixth sense, but I know Henry. He isn't someone who just falls off the map without so much as a word. If the Russians are involved, he's in real danger. I have to go back to Chicago."

"Not alone, you're not." Before she could refute him, he held up his hand. "Stop. I know you are a strong, powerful, capable cop. I get that. Good cops know when they're outgunned. I don't know much about the Russian syndicate but I'm certain you're way outgunned. Great cops know when to bring in backup. Think of Sawyer and I as yours, okay?"

Sawyer nodded. "Listen to my brother. He's right on this."

"We can work out all the details on the trip to Chicago." Reed sent her his signature wink.

"God, you're too much." She wanted to ask him about what in the hell was different now than their time on the porch when he'd given her the breathtaking good-bye kiss. Had he really changed his mind about her? This wasn't the time to delve into that. Right now she needed to find Henry and fast. "If you both insist on going, you better be ready to leave right now."

"Hold your horses." Jason shook his head. "Flowers, before you make tracks out of here, you might want to know that I do have a lead you might be interested in."

"Stop beating around the bush, Jason, and come to the point why you're here." Reed's frown screamed about his inner irritation. He grabbed her hand and gave her a reassuring squeeze.

"You and Henry really did cause quite the stir with the Russians. I was smart to have these two mavericks get you out of Destiny."

"Jason, I swear if you don't tell us what you found, I will beat it out of you." Reed's impatience seemed to be fueling his growing anger.

Jason's demeanor turned to a dark challenge. "I'd like you to try. You'd find yourself on the very wrong side of the law, Reed."

"Damn it," Nicole snapped. "I've had enough of Neanderthals. Sheriff, tell me what you know or I'm hitting the road back to Chicago right now."

"My deputy brought down a guy who was fucking with your car."

She frowned. Why would anyone mess with her car? Did Destiny have its own gang problems like back home? "That could be a coincidence, couldn't it? What would that have to do with Henry anyway?"

Jason shrugged. "Hear me out. I'm sure there's a connection. The asshole pulled a gun on Charlie."

Her jaw dropped. Apparently, Destiny was more Wild West than she'd imagined it to be. "Is he okay?"

"Yes, but he's three days from stepping down to move to California to be closer to his kids. I can't imagine how I'm going to do my job without him."

"Jason, can you stay on the topic at hand, please," Sawyer barked, his agitation obvious.

The sheriff nodded. "Sorry. Interesting thing is that even though

Charlie shot him, the creep said a few words before passing out."

"Oh my God. What happened to him?"

"The dude is alive. More flesh wound than anything, though he bled like a stuck pig. Doc is patching him up at the clinic right now. Says we should be able to talk to him in an hour or so."

"Well?" Her own impatience with the sheriff was growing just like Reed's. "What did the man say?"

"Nothing useful, but he did have a thick Russian accent." Jason smiled. "How would you like to interrogate my prisoner, Flowers?"

Real police work at last. "I would love to, Sheriff."

Chapter Thirteen

Once again, Nicole found herself in a truck between Reed, who was driving, and Sawyer, who was sitting by the passenger door. Sheriff Wolfe had given Erica a ride back into town, promising to deliver her to Dylan.

Nicole's whole life seemed to be a long, drawn-out series of mistakes. Was this another one of them?

Reed drove through the cattle guard onto the next dirt road. "Chicago, how about some music for our trip to Destiny?"

"No. The quiet is better. Helps me think." She turned to Sawyer. "This is still Stone Ranch?"

"It is," he said. "Emmett, Cody, and Bryant own a lot of acreage, but it would be bad manners to say how many."

"Seriously?" she asked.

"Yep," he said. "Let's just say they have many sections."

"Sections?"

"You forget that Nicole is a city girl, bro." Reed tapped the top of the steering wheel with his fingers. "A section is six hundred and forty acres, Chicago. The Stone brothers own nearly two hundred of them. Last time it got appraised at a quarter of a billion dollars, and that's just the land. Livestock and their other investments put them into Destiny's billionaire club."

"Shut up, Reed," Sawyer barked. "You don't know that. Emmett, Bryant, and Cody live a simple life. They don't have a mansion on O'Leary Circle, do they?"

"That doesn't mean they couldn't have one," Reed shot back. "Have you ever wanted to live in a mansion, sweetheart?"

Nicole shook her head, wondering why Reed was back to flirting and coming on strong. She was mixed up by his apparent change of heart, but that seemed to be her fallback position in any crisis. Blame everything on too much to deal with. Can't sleep? Pop your grandfather's pain pills. Too much pressure at work? More pills.

A lifetime ago she'd had goals and a plan for her span in the world. If it had panned out, she might've been awarded one or two of the many honors from the department her grandfather had earned over his long career. Granddad would've been in the audience proud as he could be. She would've married a man who would've supported her choice of a career in law enforcement. He might've even been a cop himself, but she'd actually envisioned him as a lawyer or a businessman. After she turned thirty, she and her fantasy husband would've started a family. Two kids. A boy and a girl. Later, there would've been a move to a house with four bedrooms, two baths, and a two-car garage in one of the better areas of Chicago, unlike where she'd grown up. Her kids would've gone to college and eventually started their own families. Nicole and the mirage man would've settled into retirement quite nicely—comfortable though not rich. She would've loved babysitting her grandkids.

After everything, Nicole knew that it had been only a silly fantasy. Life hadn't turned out the way she'd planned. In truth, life came at a person fast and furious, like a series of collisions, one right after the other. Flights of fancy never materialized. Feelings were overrated. Love was overrated. Believing in oneself and that anything was possible was a total waste of time and energy. With each passing mile she kept reminding herself of that fact, but with Reed's arm around her shoulder and Sawyer's hand on her knee, she was so mixed up.

"How much longer before we get to Destiny?" she asked.

"Another twenty-five minutes," Reed informed.

No time like the present to get to the bottom of what the hell Reed wanted from her. Hell, what they both wanted. If her heart was going to be destroyed, let it be now before she headed back to Chicago—

alone. "Tell me, Reed. Why the turnaround in you?"

Reed brought the truck to a stop.

"What are you doing?" she asked, feeling the pulse in her veins tighten. "I want to get to the prisoner ASAP."

"Something did go on between you two when I went to Phong's, didn't it?" Sawyer squeezed her thigh. "What did my brother say to you, baby?"

"I fucked up, bro." Reed touched her cheek, but she pulled away.

"Stop it. Both of you." She wasn't taking any more manipulation from either of them. Not any more.

"You have questions for us, Chicago." Reed's face seemed to storm with something dark and hidden. "Fire away."

"Fine. You want me to interrogate you? Then I will. You were the one who pulled back, Mr. Coleman. Not me."

"When did he do that?" Sawyer's angry tone shook her to her core.

"You were right," Reed said. "Something did happen when you were in town. Wasn't that your plan, bro? Leave us alone and let the magic take over. It worked, too."

"Then I don't understand the problem," Sawyer said.

"Neither do I," she echoed. Reed had come on so strong it nearly knocked her over. Then just as fast, he'd withdrawn from her. "If it worked then why did you make me think you were done with me?"

"I fucked up, baby. I know that. I wanted to scoop you up in my arms right then and haul you back to the bedroom and fuck you into blissful oblivion."

"Then why didn't you?"

"I should have. I may never forgive myself for not doing just that, but I'm saying it now, baby. I want you."

"You've got to understand him, Nicole," Sawyer said in a low, gentle tone. "He took our parents' death harder than anyone."

"She's got her own demons, brother. I have no excuse for pushing her away." Reed cupped her chin. "If you'll let me, I *will* make up for my mistake. I would like you to stay in Destiny with Sawyer and me. That's what I want, Nicole. What do you want?"

She would've liked to believe him, believe in the new dream, the one with her being loved and cherished by these two incredible men. Magic wasn't real. If there was any chance of her heart healing one day, it was time to end whatever this was before it went on any longer. "Reed, I told you my deepest, darkest secrets." She turned to Sawyer. "You deserve to know the truth about me, too. I'm a recovering addict. I was benched because of a mistake I made two years ago. I'm no super cop. I work a desk back at the station. I'm nothing more than a paper shuffler. I've seen the look in your eyes. I'm not the woman you think I am. I never will be."

"Not true, Nicole." Sawyer touched her cheek. "Not true at all. You're everything I've ever wanted and more. What are you afraid of? The poly life? I know you're not from here but you have to believe me when I say it is a great life. Are you fearful that Reed and I will get jealous, that each of us will want you for ourselves? It won't happen. Our dads gave us the perfect example of how to treat a woman. You're the one for us. Trust me."

She crossed her arms over her chest, trying to create a kind of defensive barrier between them and her. *I can't be the woman who tears them apart. I won't be.* "Reed says he's into me now, but what about later?"

"What do you mean, baby?" Reed asked.

"You two are into BDSM. The club in Destiny, Phase Four, that's your club. You've shared women before, right?"

They both shrugged, but she could tell they had and probably numerous times.

"Those women were into the life, too, right?"

"Yes, but I don't see how that means a fucking thing about if you should stay in Destiny with us or not." Reed's temper was rising and fast, boiling over, creating an edge in his voice that made her anxious.

There was no turning back now. Summoning all her will to the forefront, she hit the one button in Reed she'd felt from him on the porch. "I've never tried even light BDSM. I've never even fantasized about it. Will you still want me if I can't get into it?"

The dark burn she'd seen on Reed's face vanished, but he didn't answer her, instead remaining silent. She'd plainly gotten to the crux of the issue that was impenetrable in him.

"Of course we want you," Sawyer said. "For you, Nicole, I would move heaven and earth. If you don't like the life, then I will walk away from it. Being a Dom is only one facet of who I am."

She grabbed his hand. "For you, yes. I believe you would do exactly what you're saying, Sawyer. But what about Reed?"

"What about me?"

"Can you honestly tell me that you would walk away from your lifestyle just to have a chance with me? I tried to talk to you about BDSM. You answered a few questions but you kept changing the subject. Why? Because, unlike Sawyer, being a Dom is part of you as much as being a cowboy."

Without warning, Reed kissed her, tracing her lips with his tongue, causing her pulse to burn and her skin to tingle. He released her lips. "Yes. I would give it up for you, Chicago."

She closed her eyes, knowing he was telling the truth and feeling her heart swell in her chest. "But it's not right for me to ask you to do that, Reed."

"I think you're getting ahead of yourself, sweetheart."

"What do you mean?"

"First, you said it yourself that you haven't given much thought to our ways. Why would you? You never had a reason to until now. Second, you don't get to decide what is right for me. I do that. Third, I want you, Nicole. I've never known anyone like you. Sawyer may be able to get into people's head and figure out what they are thinking before they say a word, but he doesn't get me the way you do. No one ever has before. That was the real reason I froze on the back porch earlier. I wasn't sure how to handle that. I know now."

"I'm so mixed up," she confessed. "How can this even be possible?" She brought her hands up to her eyes, which were filling with fresh tears.

Sawyer stroked her hair, "Sweetheart, take your time."

"That's just it. We don't have time. I need to talk to Jason's prisoner. Then I need to get back to Chicago. I know you said you were going with me but do you really think that's a good idea? Reed, you deserve a woman who can be all you need. I'm not sure that's me."

"I'm sure. You've got to trust me about that, Chicago. I know you're worried about not being comfortable with BDSM." Reed feathered his fingertips up and down her arm. "Stop worrying. In many ways that's at the center of our lifestyle, baby. Doms create a space for a woman to just be, to embrace her feminine side fully, to trust her deepest instincts, and to really feel pleasure."

That sounded amazing to her. Had she ever experienced anything like that in her life? Never. "Quite the pitch, Reed."

"Not a pitch, baby. I feel like you will enjoy our ways more than you can imagine."

"I sense that, too, Nicole." Sawyer's tone was deep and confident.

"You do?"

He nodded.

Reed continued, "If it turns out you can't embrace BDSM, so be it. I never saw myself living a vanilla life, but if that's what you need, I will be the most vanilla guy in all of Colorado. You'll see."

She smiled, feeling her ancient fears crumbling inside her. Still, a few shreds remained. "Two against one isn't a fair fight, guys. Don't you think we're all being foolish about this? We're all talking like we've settled into something permanent. Not quite a 'love at first sight' fling but not far from it either. How is that even possible in the short time we've known each other?"

"You mean you didn't want me the first time you saw me, baby?" Reed was teasing her.

"I thought you both were incredibly sexy, but that was the extent of it. What about you, Reed? I could see in your eyes lust, but you didn't want more did you? How can you know you want to pursue a relationship with me already? We all got lost in the moment. That's all." She hated her words but she could not deny the logic.

"Do you remember what the fortune from Phong's cookie was? It said, 'Happiness is right in front of you.' You're my happiness. I didn't believe I would ever feel this way. My parents' death changed me, made me hard. You, Nicole Flowers, have broken through all my walls. My brother and sister never could do that, but you did. You. I can't get over how courageous you are."

"I'm not courageous, Reed."

"Yes you are," he said. "You're a cop through and through, but you're also a woman."

Sawyer cupped her chin. "I think you've had to be tough for so long you've lost sight of that, haven't you, sweetheart?"

She sighed and felt her shoulders sag. "My whole life has been one long series of fights. I can't be vulnerable. Whenever I've allowed myself to be feminine, to be exposed, everything has come crashing down around me. I've learned to expect disappointment. Being with you at the cabin was amazing, but can you honestly tell me we that we can beat the odds? The rule for me has always been to embrace the old saying of 'all good things must come to an end.'"

"Me, too, baby. Sawyer and I have suffered loss. You have suffered loss. It's time to grab on to each other and enjoy the next chapters of the rest of our lives." Reed planted his mouth on hers, and she felt her heart rush to him. His tongue swept along the ridge of her lips and then plunged in.

She was filled with happiness as Reed's mouth left her and was instantly replaced by Sawyer's. Her toes curled as he claimed her with his lips and invading tongue.

Sweet emotions of acceptance were racing through her, blossoming into a warming sensation throughout her body. The kissing session continued for a few minutes until her lips throbbed deliciously.

When it ended, her cowboys looked at her with hazy, warm eyes.

Then a buzzing sound pulled her back. It came from her cell in her jacket.

"Leave it, baby," Reed said.

"You know I can't do that." She pulled out the cell and looked at the screen. The call was from Jason. "Can we table this discussion for later?" Not waiting for an answer and happy to have a moment to catch her breath, she clicked the green "talk" button. "Hello, Sheriff. We'll be there in a few minutes."

"I'm at the jail," Jason said.

"I thought the guy was at the clinic."

"He is. Charlie is there, making sure he stays put. Shouldn't be a problem since the doc is keeping the prick sedated. Come to the jail first."

She was about to ask him why when the call dropped. "Damn." Clicking the call back button didn't reconnect the call. "We've got to go."

"Okay, but we're not finished talking," Sawyer said.

"You're right about that, brother." Reed turned the key in the ignition and fired up the engine. "She's still holding back, right?"

"Yep. I think your intuition is as good as mine lately."

"Only with her," Reed said, driving them down the road.

The hours with them had flown by. Never had Nicole's emotions been so raw, causing her head to spin and her heart to race. She no longer doubted Reed's intent. As much as Sawyer wanted something more permanent from her, so did he. But she couldn't see how it would work. They were both ready to toss the life they'd known their entire adult lives for her. There was no way she would ask them to do that. Besides, there would eventually be a time when they would regret their choice.

She needed to remain focused on finding Henry. That needed to be her only goal, even though her heart was trying to shove her into the arms of these beautiful cowboys.

I've got two amazing men who want me and God knows I want them. What's wrong with me?

She closed her eyes and felt the hard truth swirl in her head. Reed and Sawyer deserved better than her, better than a fuckup, an addict.

Chapter Fourteen

Topping the rise on Turkey Pass five miles from the Silver Spoon Bridge into Destiny, Sawyer saw black smoke coming from somewhere in the town. "Oh shit. Do you see that?"

"Yep," Reed said. "Chicago, we've got to make a detour to the firehouse."

"Reed and I are volunteer firefighters, sweetheart," he added.

"Of course. No problem," Nicole answered. "Can you tell what's on fire from here?"

"No. It looks bad though." Reed increased the speed of the truck, clearly wanting to get to the action fast. "Whatever is on fire is in the northeast part of town."

Sawyer knew Destiny like the back of his hand. That could be any number of homes or businesses. Blue's Diner. The Dream Hotel. Or the clinic—the place they were going to join Jason and meet up with Charlie to question the prisoner. He had a bad feeling in the pit of his stomach that their detour wasn't a detour at all.

* * * *

Nicole watched the dark smoke contaminating the blue Colorado sky.

Reed brought the truck to a sudden stop, unable to go farther up West Street due to the blockade in the road. "Sawyer, there's Jason."

"I see him."

So did Nicole. The sheriff was rushing to secure the area.

She and her cowboys jumped out of the truck. They ran up to

Sheriff Wolfe, who was dragging sawhorses into the road with the help of a few people. She recognized a couple of them. Dylan wore his signature sunglasses, dark suit, and black tie. If anyone looked like a government agent or spy, it was that man. Alexei, the former mob assassin turned good guy, was taking control of the crowd with only gestures and a few simple words. Impressive.

"Jason, we need someone to protect Nicole so we can get to fighting the fire," Reed said as they approached the sheriff.

"Shit. Yes. You both are the only certified guys on the squad." The sheriff motioned Dylan and Alexei closer.

"I don't need bodyguards," she snapped. "I can be of use here."

"Not a chance," Sawyer said. "We know that one Russian came to Destiny and messed with your car. Who knows how many more might be coming?"

"There's Dylan's brother, Cam. Erica is with him." Reed pointed to a large man standing next to his sister about ten feet away from them. Cam's eyes never left Erica. "He can help, too. He's an attorney here in Destiny and one of the best shots in the whole state."

"This is ridiculous. I don't need an attorney or bodyguards or babysitters." Nicole felt her heart racing. "Sawyer, you're not in charge. I have experience in this kind of situation. I can help."

"Flowers, I am in charge here." Jason shook his head. "You'll be most helpful if you cooperate. We don't know if the Russian we caught was working alone or not. I'm sure you're very capable, but you don't know anyone in Destiny besides Reed and Sawyer. It's too big of a risk."

"You're making a mistake, Sheriff. I know how to handle a crowd."

"I have a pretty good idea you do." Jason's steady gaze reminded her of her grandfather. The one thing she and the sheriff had in common was duty. "I would be frustrated, too, if I were in your shoes, but we must be very careful at this point. With all this excitement, you would be an easy target, Nicole."

She shrugged. "Don't you need all the volunteers you can get on this? I'm a seasoned officer."

"We're not going to lose you now, baby," Sawyer said. "We just found you."

Her training disagreed with him, but her heart understood he was right. "Okay. I'll stay put."

"It would be best to get your woman into an enclosed space that I can secure. We can take Erica with us, too," Dylan said.

Nicole shook her head and opened her jacket to reveal her holstered gun underneath. "I'm not helpless."

"Clearly not," the sheriff said. "I've asked a couple of citizens to keep everyone in the park." He turned to Dylan. "Use Father Dragon and the big pine tree by his statue as cover. That leaves only a few spaces you'll have to keep your eyes on. She'll be safe there."

"That statue in the park is an additional half block away from the fire. I won't be able to see a thing from there. By these sawhorses, I can at least see what's going on, and if I'm needed I can be of some help." She folded her arms over her chest in defiance. "I let you guys win the war, but I demand to win this battle."

"Demand?" Reed's eyebrows shot up.

"We don't have time for this," Jason barked. "Either give in or don't. We've got to get to the fire." The sheriff didn't wait to find out what they would decide but ran down the street toward the clinic.

"Done. You can stay here, Nicole, but no closer." Sawyer turned to Dylan, Alexei, and Cam. "Keep your eyes wide open. Your new client is precious to us."

Then he and Reed bolted the same direction Jason had run—to the fire.

* * * *

Reed and Sawyer finished putting on their firefighting gear. The entire two-story clinic was ablaze. Out of every window on its second floor the blackest smoke Reed had ever seen billowed out. Red and orange flames licked the broken glass of the first floor windows and doors.

The Knight brothers, Eric and Scott, the acting EMTs on the scene, checked the lucky victims' vitals. The survivors' words couldn't be heard over Destiny's lone fire engine moan, Old Red's siren.

Jason came up to him and Sawyer. "Eight unaccounted for. Doc Ryder, two nurses, four patients—one of whom was the Russian Flowers wants to question, and Charlie."

Reed shook his head thinking of Nicole and glad she was safe back at the barricade with the three capable men around her. He wished it could be him, but he and Sawyer were needed here. Then his mind snapped to the last time he'd talked to Charlie Blake, Destiny's favorite deputy sheriff. Charlie and the others were inside the burning clinic. Reed turned to Sawyer. "Let's go."

* * * *

Nicole was a total bundle of nerves. Her eyes hadn't left Reed and Sawyer since they'd run down the street to the disaster. Even from this distance, she could see them, which made her feel a tiny bit better. Suddenly, she watched them run into the burning building. Her heart stopped.

She felt an arm come around her shoulder.

"It's going to be okay," a woman's voice said. "Reed and Sawyer will be fine. You'll see."

She turned to the blonde woman. "I hope you're right. I just feel so helpless."

"I've been there. I know the feeling, and it sucks. But trust me, it's going to be okay. Eric and Scott are volunteer EMTs. They're helping with the fire, too. They're my guys." The kind lady, Nicole guessed to be in her mid-twenties, stood with a few of Destiny's citizens that had been allowed closer to the action. The rest were on the northwest corner of the town's park. Everyone, including her, was in shock at the destruction they were witnessing. "I'm Megan."

"Nicole."

Megan smiled broadly. "Everyone in Destiny knows who you are, Nicole."

"They do."

"I'm still getting used to this town, but you'll come to love it like I have."

"I'm only here for a week or two, Megan. No more."

"That's what I thought when I came here." The blonde squeezed her tight. "You might be surprised."

Even surrounded by other onlookers, she felt so alone. Her three newly appointed bodyguards had gone into action in a flash after her cowboys and Jason had left, stepping away into the background to remain inconspicuous. The three men weren't quite invisible but close.

Alexei stood twenty feet away in front of Blue's Diner, constantly scanning the area for any trouble. She found it ironic that one of her protectors against the Russian mob was a former Russian mobster himself.

Dylan was closest to her of the three. He stood about four feet to her right still wearing his dark sunglasses. Law enforcement was something she'd been around since childhood, but Strange was unlike anyone she'd ever known. His intensity was substantial.

Dylan and Alexei clearly had experience in covert operations. Cam, not so much.

Even though they were brothers, Cam and Dylan had completely different personalities. Dylan was a cool operator. Cam seemed almost manic and argumentative. Dylan's tool of choice clearly was his gun. Standing across the street where Dylan had sent him and Erica, Cam held his tool of choice, his cell. He held it to his ear, but the majority of his focus clearly remained on Reed and Sawyer's lovely sister as his eyes never left her. Being an attorney, maybe he was dealing with a big case. She wasn't sure, but still felt Cam's frame and height would intimidate just about anybody.

Nicole looked back at the smoke above the clinic. She prayed silently, "Please God, let Reed and Sawyer be safe."

* * * *

Sawyer knew fighting a fire was part science and part luck. Flames were consuming the walls of the clinic's lobby, as he and Reed fought to contain the blaze.

This disaster was the worst the Fire Squad had faced in town ever. Even though the risk had been high, he and Reed had gone into the burning structure because eight souls were still inside. Cody Stone had joined them, leaving the other volunteers to man the hoses and fight the fire from outside.

Sawyer would bet this had been an act of arson, though he had no proof of it yet. If he was right, it meant Nicole, the woman of his dreams, needed protection from the Russians. It would be only a matter of time before they came for her. He regretted not going along with Dylan's suggestion of pulling her into a secure room. Once done here, he would make sure to do whatever it took to keep her safe.

"Guys, over here," Reed yelled.

* * * *

Nicole could taste the acid from the fumes of the fire on her lips. She couldn't imagine what Reed and Sawyer were dealing with inside the structure. She could see the flames coming out of the upper floor's windows. She had to remind herself to keep breathing.

More people were joining the rest of the onlookers, but most were silent as they gawked at the blaze. The few words uttered came from two silver-haired women a few feet in front of her.

"My God, did everyone get out safe, Ethel?" one of the senior ladies said in a distinct British accent.

"No word yet, Gretchen," Ethel answered, looking at her cell's screen.

A couple of men rushed past her.

"Where are you going?" she shouted to them, unable to not take charge, despite Wolfe's earlier demand.

"We're volunteers, miss," one of them yelled back over his shoulder. He knocked over one of the sawhorses, but didn't stop.

She glanced around for anyone suspicious looking, anyone with a gun barrel pointed her direction. When none was found, she moved to the downed sawhorse and sat it back up. Wolfe would have to understand her training had kicked into high gear during this emergency. She wasn't going to be stupid though. Truthfully, she was glad that Dylan and Alexei were there with her, watching her back.

She remained on the other side of the blockade, which granted her an extra six inches closer to the blaze. Turning around to face the fire, she had a much clearer view of what was happening at the clinic.

Her heart wasn't here. It was inside the burning building.

Nicole hoped for everyone's safety, but especially for Sawyer's and Reed's.

* * * *

With Reed's mind on his task but also on Nicole, he entered the hallway, which looked like the throat of a fire-breathing dragon. Sawyer and Cody followed close behind. Together, they were able to clear a path to the rooms in the back. They didn't have much time. There was no way the clinic would survive this. He looked into the first room. Paris, a young nurse at the clinic, was crouched on the floor. Her violet eyes were wide with fear.

"You okay?" Reed asked her while Cody and Sawyer doused the area around the door with retardant foam.

She nodded.

"Where are the rest?"

The nurse coughed and pointed down the hallway where the fire was even stronger.

"I'm going to carry you out, understand?" Reed asked.

Close to passing out, Paris nodded. He lifted her up over his shoulders in the traditional fireman's carry.

"I'll get her out to the EMTs," he told Cody and Sawyer, praying they'd find more survivors. "I'll be back to help you with the others as fast as I can."

With a single nod, Sawyer went deeper into the monster's belly with Cody.

Reed carried Paris to safety.

* * * *

Filled with anxiety, Nicole turned to Ethel, one of the few who had moved closer to the barriers with her, "Any word yet?"

Staring at her cellphone's screen, Ethel shook her head.

Gretchen frowned. "You think that you being the county judge would give you firsthand info."

"One would think, but not true in this kind of situation," Ethel answered, nose down in her phone.

Nicole balled up her fists. Not being a person who sat back and let things just happen, her insides were pushing her to act.

Dylan stepped next to her. "I know that look, Flowers, but you're staying here. You're only half a block away now. You have a clear shot of everything going on at the fire. No closer. Or I can accompany you to the jail." He faced her but his eyes were hidden behind his Aviators. "This isn't your beat back in Chicago."

She thought about correcting him—telling him she no longer had a beat but instead a desk—but didn't. The no-nonsense man wasn't going to be persuaded to change his mind, of that she was sure.

Then she saw one of the firemen come out of the building with a woman on his shoulders. Even from this distance, Nicole knew it was Reed. A little relief rolled through her.

"Look," a woman to the side of her said, pointing at the clinic. The flames, which had been seen from the upper floor windows, were now coming from the lower ones as well.

Nicole gasped as Reed handed the woman over to the medical personal and headed back into the burning building to join Sawyer, who was still inside.

* * * *

Sawyer handed over the latest survivor they'd found—Katy, another nurse—to Eric to assess her injuries. Five had been rescued by him, Reed, and Cody already, but three more were yet to be found—Doc Ryder, Charlie, and the Russian. They had ten more rooms left to check, and those were all on the part of the top floor that was getting the worst of the blaze.

He rushed back in to join Reed and Cody to continue their rescue operation.

* * * *

Nicole had seen Reed and Sawyer bring out more people from the blaze only to return back into the monster. Keeping her eyes fixed on the clinic, she was still aware of Gretchen and Ethel, who were handing out water to people near her by the sawhorses. Back in the park, she'd heard others were doing the same there for the bigger crowd. The local restaurateurs had brought the bottles for everyone since the temperature had risen several degrees due to the blaze.

Her law enforcement training was in high gear. Though the bulk of her attention was on the fire, she was keeping a close watch out of the corner of her eyes at everything going on around her. No Russians yet. Two beautiful women stood on either side of a young Hispanic boy. One of the women had long auburn hair and the other had blonde.

"Nicole, have you met Amber?" Ethel put her hand on the auburn-haired beauty. Clearly everyone, including the county judge, was trying to distract themselves from the tragedy, but failing miserably. "Or are you going by Kathy White these days, Amber?"

"Just Amber, Judge." The woman extended her hand to Nicole. "I haven't had the pleasure."

Kathy White? The missing person on the report. Nicole felt her heart skip a beat.

"I'm Nicole Flowers." She took Amber's hand. "Nice to meet you."

"This is my sister Belle." Amber motioned to the blonde woman. Then she put her arm around the boy. "And this handsome devil is Juan."

"Hi Juan," Nicole said, giving him her best smile despite her current state of worry.

"Are you the policewoman from Chicago who Mama Belle and everyone have been talking about?"

"Juan, that's rude." Belle shook her head.

"Sorry, Mama."

"To Miss Flowers, young man."

"Sorry, Miss Flowers."

"Nothing to be sorry about." Glancing back at the fire every few seconds, Nicole leaned down in front of Juan until they were at eye level with each other. "I am from Chicago and I am a police officer."

He smiled broadly. "*Magnifico.* Do you like our town, Miss Flowers?"

"Very much, Juan."

Gretchen turned to Amber and Belle. "I bet it was arson."

"Don't go starting rumors until the official word is out," Ethel scolded.

"You'll see I'm right," Gretchen answered.

Arson? Nicole's gut twisted into a knot of fresh worry for Reed and Sawyer.

* * * *

With Sawyer and Cody close behind, Reed inched his way forward through the haze of black into the final room they would be able to check. They should've already called it a loss and pulled back. This floor was going to give way to the bottom of the building any minute. Spotting three unmoving forms in the room, Reed held on to a sliver of hope but mostly expected the worst.

"I got this one," he said, moving to the unconscious person on his left. Charlie. He looked bad. Real bad.

"Mine." Sawyer took the one to the right. "This is Doc. He's breathing."

Cody went to the Russian on the bed.

Each of them hauled one of the men onto their shoulders and rushed out the room.

A sudden explosion knocked them off their feet and the floor collapsed. Falling, Reed's thoughts were of Nicole only and how much he wanted to hold her again.

* * * *

All the blood in Nicole's veins turned to ice as an explosion at the clinic shook the ground under her feet. *Sawyer and Reed are still in there!*

She fought back the tears, trying to convince herself those amazing men were safe and would be headed her way soon.

Though the people around her were clearly in shock given their collective gasps and whispered questions to each other, she couldn't move her attention away from the flame-engulfed structure.

Sawyer and Reed had been wonderful to her. They'd made her feel alive, really alive, maybe for the first time in her life. They were incredible, loving men. Charming. Funny. Warm. She'd brought this hell to them by insisting on coming here to look into the error on the Missing Person's Report. Had Nicole's desire to try to clear her name and Henry's brought *her* bad luck to Destiny somehow? God, if she could only take it back. But she couldn't. She tried to calm her mind. Her cowboys had to be okay. They must. She wrung her hands, waiting for the official word to come. She'd already fallen for Sawyer and Reed hard. How would she survive without them? The answer was—she wouldn't.

"Ethel, get on that thing and find out what the bloody hell just happened." Gretchen looked stricken, as her friend, also white as a ghost, nodded.

Ethel punched a number on her cell and then brought it up to her ear. "It's ringing."

Nicole could feel her heart beating in her chest. Maybe they went out the back of the building. *Please be okay. Please.*

"Patrick. Thank God. What happened down there? No." Ethel shook her head and said quietly, "The second floor collapsed?"

Oh God!

"Ask him if any—" Gretchen said.

Ethel held up her hand, which was shaking. Everyone seemed to hold his or her breath, hoping for news. "Yes. Okay. Okay. I love you, too." She clicked off the phone and addressed the crowd in a steady, authoritative tone. "Folks, please remain calm. At this point they do not know what caused the fire or what exploded. They are working to control the fire so it doesn't spread to the hotel or other buildings nearby."

"My house is on the opposite corner of McDavish and Big Elm," someone said. "Is it okay?"

"So far only the clinic is in danger," Ethel informed.

"What about the patients inside the clinic," a man to the back of the throng shouted. "Is anyone hurt?"

"No news on that, but my husband Patrick just told me they would be sending someone to us with an update shortly."

"Ethel, you're not just stalling are you?" Gretchen asked quietly but loud enough for Nicole and those closest to hear.

The judge shook her head. "Six were still inside when the explosion happened."

Six? God, don't let it be them.

Nicole swallowed hard, trying to quell the dread wrapping its claws around her throat. Being positive was never something that came natural to her. She was more of an expect-the-worst-and-you'll-never-be-disappointed kind of girl. Right now, she wanted to be the opposite but was having a difficult time turning her old habit around.

A figure in full fire gear ran toward them from the clinic. Nicole could instantly tell by the person's height they weren't either Reed or Sawyer, both of whom had a full six or more inches on this one.

When the firefighter removed his hat, Nicole realized this person was a woman. The firefighter's long, dark hair spilled down to her shoulders. Her lips were red and her eyes were deep blue.

"Phoebe, what's the news?" Amber asked the question everyone was longing to have answered.

Breathing hard, Phoebe took a bottle of water and downed half of it. "I've got news," she said between more sips and breaths.

"Spill it, counselor," Ethel ordered.

"It's not good. Looks like the clinic will be a total loss."

"Was anyone hurt?" Nicole asked, fearing what the truth might be.

Phoebe closed her eyes. "It's bad," she choked out.

Her insides tightened into a horrific knot. She'd never let her attention move from the clinic, hoping against hope for two figures to emerge from the blaze. They hadn't.

Nicole wanted to scream, wanted to run, wanted to pound her fists on something hard until they bled.

Chapter Fifteen

Nicole's head swam as she stared at Phoebe. "Who? Are Reed and Sawyer okay?" The pit in her stomach tightened like a vise.

"They're fine. Heroes even. Ask anyone."

"Thank God." Nicole felt relief spread through her. *They're okay.* Her cowboys were safe.

"They were inside when the floor collapsed but their firefighting expertise ended up saving their lives and others. They were able to escape out the back."

That's why I didn't see them.

"Doc is in bad shape but Eric and Scott are with him. I think he will pull through. The Russian guy is dead. Smoke inhalation got him." Phoebe closed her eyes and sighed. "Charlie didn't make it, though. He was unresponsive when they found him." Then she choked out, "Charlie died as they were carrying him out."

Nicole's own eyes brimmed with tears. The only time she'd been around the deputy was on her first day in Destiny. Nicole wished she could've known him better. Charlie seemed like a very nice man and a good cop.

"Not Charlie." Ethel shook her head and her lips quivered. "He was only a few days away from seeing his kids again."

Wiping the tears from her eyes, Ethel put her arm around Gretchen, who was weeping, too. Amber, Belle, and Phoebe were also expressing sadness and holding on to each other in an attempt to soften the blow.

Nicole had never seen a place like Destiny, where people felt for each other so deeply and honestly. Being a neighbor here meant something. This lovely respite from her life had been wonderful, but it was only a dream. Reality waited for her return to her desk. She would hate to leave it, having already fallen for two of its sons, but she must. Her case had blown up and brought tragedy to Destiny. Better to keep the Russian mob in Chicago than out here. With Reed and Sawyer safely out of harm's way, it was past time for her to go back to where she belonged.

"Flowers, you look like person who just ate bad Solyanka," Alexei said to her, pulling her back from the women who were trying to console each other over the loss of one of their own.

"What?"

"Solyanka. Sour soup. You have tried? No? Probably for best." Alexei's odd speech didn't put her off. In fact it held an endearing quality. "I see much on face of yours. Mitrofanov man death troubles you, yes?"

She nodded. "I might've gotten something I could've used to clear my friend back in Chicago." *Henry? God, where could he be?* "Now, I'm back at square one."

Alexei frowned. "Square one?"

"I have to start over on my case."

"Ah. Square one. Yes. I understand. I have information to help with case of yours, Nicole. Square two."

"What do you know?" Nicole hoped it was something useful, something that would lead her to Henry's whereabouts.

"I tell CIA agent already. He does not tell you?" Alexei pointed to Dylan.

"Former," Dylan corrected. "We should wait for a better time when the sheriff is here, Markov. And we definitely shouldn't discuss this in the open."

Alexei snorted. "Why?" He looked around the area. "No Russians here, CIA. Only citizens of US." Alexei pointed to his own chest. "American. Safe to talk."

"Tell me what you know, right now," Nicole demanded.

"The lady wants to know, CIA. Her I tell now. Mitrofanov send only one direct report to here for you. Niklaus is be keeping someone in his pants at your station back in Chicago."

"What?" she asked, shaking her head. "Why would he have someone in his…pocket. You meant pocket. For a minute I thought I had a much bigger problem. Yes. I already know about that."

"Word on streets is Niklaus's insider be very nervous. I hate to say this. It is hard thing. Do you think about fact that this man in pocket is Henry? I know he is being your friend, but I have many suspicions."

Henry? She couldn't believe he would be involved with the Russians. It just didn't fit his personality. "It's not Henry."

Alexei shrugged. "I would be placing bet that insider is worried you have evidence to make charges that stick to him and Niklaus."

"I don't."

"Yes, but this is not what Mitrofanov's man thinks. He thinks you are singing like the pigeons. You know what happens to many singing pigeons in prisons." Alexei took his thumb and traced it across his throat. "They make the pigeons dead. Are you understanding, Nicole?"

"Yes, I get you. Sort of." If Henry was the insider, God forbid, Nicole had to find him before Niklaus did. She owed him and the memory of her grandfather at least that. "All the more reason to get back to Chicago."

"Maybe," Alexei said. "Or maybe we should be setting trap for insider here."

"In Destiny?" She nodded, believing Henry wasn't involved. "How?"

"In this case, truth is best. Sheriff will call. He will ask why a Chicago police officer is asking questions about a closed case."

She nodded. "That should get people hopping."

"You are suspended. They must to investigate. Your commander will put a team together. The real mole will pass on information to

Russians. Though the mole will likely look more like badger. I have long argument with partner. Stubborn man, but he insist I call mole and he has tranquilizer gun. So the mole badger will tell Russians. They will send someone here hoping to cover all of the tracks. We trap hit man. Unless he actually looks like mole. Then I step on him. You see my point? At least badger has claws. This is faulty metaphor."

Dear God, she had to stop him now. "How do we get the hit man to talk?"

Alexei sent his left fist into his right palm with a smack. "I know how to get people to be talking. We have many ways. The Mitrofanov man will lead us to mole."

"So you want to use me as bait?" Could her commander be the mole? Maybe.

"You should not to be worrying about this. You have two capable bodyguards and you have gun of your own. I suspect you know how to use."

"Yes." Sawyer and Reed might not think she could handle a weapon given the moth incident, but she knew she could. She grinned. "I'm a good shot, Alexei."

Alexei smiled. "Get rat to poke head around Destiny, then we pounce. Sheriff might frown on idea, but will work. Rat. See, rat is better than mole. Mole is blind. No one is afraid of mole."

Sheriff Wolfe, for all his words, hadn't been treating her like an equal, like a fellow officer. Alexei seemed more inclined to trust her with such a dangerous mission. That pleased her. It made her feel like a real cop again.

His idea wasn't bad, and it would allow her a few more days with Reed and Sawyer.

Not a bad idea at all. "Make the call, Alexei."

If they could trap the real insider, she had a better chance of finding Henry. Her thoughts were on Reed and Sawyer. She turned her attention back toward the clinic for any sign of them.

Chapter Sixteen

Sawyer didn't wait to shed the rest of his fire gear, and neither did Reed. They both ran down West Street to Nicole, who was standing by the sawhorses Jason had put up as a blockade. Even though exhausted from fighting the blaze, the relief of seeing her safe and sound gave him and obviously Reed, too, a much needed boost of energy.

"She's okay," Sawyer panted out.

"Thank God," Reed responded.

Standing near Nicole, along with other Destonians, were the three bodyguards they'd entrusted with her safety—Dylan and Cam Strange, and the Russian consultant, Alexei Markov. Those three men had earned his utmost respect. He wasn't sure how to repay them, but he would do his damnedest to find a way.

"Nicole," he shouted.

She ran past the sawhorses and they met in the middle of the street. He and Reed wrapped her up in their arms.

Nicole's whole body was shaking and tears were streaming out of her eyes. "You're safe. You're okay."

Reed kissed her first. "So are you, Chicago. So are you."

Tell her Reed. Tell her how you feel.

But Sawyer was certain his brother was still struggling with how to voice those three words that came so hard for him ever since their parents' death. Reed clearly needed more time to speak his true feelings to Nicole.

She turned to him. "Sawyer, your face is covered in soot. Did the medical guys check you two out already?"

He cupped her chin. "No, sweetheart. I couldn't wait to see you. I wanted to make sure the woman I loved was safe."

She smiled broadly and kissed him. Then she glanced over at Reed.

Tell her now, bro.

"Nicole, want to come with us while we get looked over by the EMTs?" Reed definitely wasn't ready yet.

"I would love to go with you," Nicole said. "It will make me feel better to hear the official word on your health."

"You heard the lady," his brother said to him. "Let's go."

They placed her between them, Reed's arm around her shoulders and his around her waist.

"I want to hear everything that happened in the clinic, guys," she told them, assuming her law enforcement demeanor once again. God, everything about her was so incredibly sexy.

"You will, Chicago," Reed said as they headed back to the EMTs.

Sawyer could see such hope in both of them. They had a lot in common. Together, they could find comfort and a future with his help. He wasn't about to lose Nicole, so he silently vowed to do whatever it took to get Reed and her to open up and be honest with each other—and with him.

* * * *

Reed sat in the booth by the center window of Lucy's Burgers with Nicole and Sawyer across from him. It was their latest stop in Alexei's intricate trap. Against his and Sawyer's better judgment, they were following the former mobster's plan to the letter to fool the Mitrofanov's insider. Dylan and Jason had deputized several citizens to be close at all times. Though a good step, it hadn't swayed him or Sawyer into going along with the idea. Nicole's safety meant everything to them, and her touring the town alone to flush out the rat was too dangerous. What had pushed them to give in was Nicole's insistence to try Alexei's trap combined with the agreement by all parties that he and Sawyer could be at Nicole's side at all times, play-acting as tour guides instead of their real job as her bodyguards.

Alexei's plan was very precise and tiring. Every second of the day was scheduled. Most thought it was the only way to get the job done right.

This was only day two.

Everyone but her believed the insider was Henry Underwood, and most thought he was going to show up here in Destiny soon to get her. Playing superspy in town didn't fit into what Reed wanted. What he really desired was to go back up the mountain to his beloved Coleman Territory and get inside the cabin with Nicole. Even though he and Sawyer were getting to spend time with her, it wasn't under the best conditions. How could it be with so many of Dylan's overzealous Destonian recruits for this project—*to catch a mole*—always so close and in earshot*?*

"Where are we supposed to go after this?" Sawyer motioned Lucy over for a refill of tea.

How that woman could twirl her Hula-hoop around her waist through the tiny aisle without knocking over customers' dishes had always been a mystery to Reed.

Nicole checked the iPad, which had Alexei's plan spelled out for them. TBK's newest programmers, Sean MacCabe and Matt Dixon, had added a tracking device to it. Dylan trusted the two Texans, having worked with them when he was at the CIA. The addition to the tablet was so that if anything went wrong, Jason and Dylan could still find them.

Nicole read off their next stop on the iPad. "Central Park by the Red Dragon for a picnic. Chinese food from Phong's."

"Not again. We had that yesterday, too." Sawyer groaned. "My horse is going to buck my fat ass off when I get back to the ranch if Alexei doesn't come up with something other than eating to flush out the insider."

She smiled. "I like Chinese, and Phong's is the best I've ever had."

Reed moved his hand into his front pocket to touch the fortune he'd gotten his first meal with Nicole. When his finger touched the edge of the slip of paper, he quietly pulled his hand out.

Happiness is right in front of you.

Yes, she is.

His plate had the hand-cut French fries and double cheeseburger he loved. Just getting a whiff of his favorite meal here would have his mouth drooling normally. But even though two days had passed since the fire, his nose still only detected noxious smoke.

Doc Ryder was recovering nicely at the courthouse, which had been set up as a temporary hospital. He'd filled them in on the events that led up to the moment the fire started. He and Charlie had gone into the Russian's room and found him with his hands on an oxygen tank's open valve. The gas was on fire and had already spread to the walls. The doc had spotted a discarded Zippo on the floor that told him the fucker had set the blaze. How the man had gotten his hands on an oxygen tank and a lighter was still a mystery. Doc and Charlie had worked together to secure the creep to the bed. They'd even gotten the valve closed on the tank, but it had been too late to stop the blaze. The fire had spread out of the room and into the hallway, blocking their only exit.

The preliminary findings also showed that the explosion that had come later, destroying the second floor, had been the result of the fire spreading to the closet that held more tanks of gas.

Reed looked down at his plate and shook his head. It would likely be several more days before his smeller got back to functioning properly.

Unlike Sawyer, he could always make room for more food. Put it in front of him and he would eat it, hungry or not. "How long before this Henry guy shows? I'm tired of this act." Reed took a bite of the cheeseburger, chewing on the flat-tasting sandwich. Apparently flavor resided more in the nose than on the tongue. "This is so bland." He leaned across the table and placed both hands on the sides of Nicole's face. "I know you taste better than anything I've ever had on my lips before." He kissed her, sending his tongue into her sweet mouth. The feel of her quivering lips made him instantly hard. *Damn, I want to get you up to my cabin.* He leaned back and enjoyed the look of her reddening cheeks.

"Reed, everyone is watching us," Nicole whispered.

Reed looked around the restaurant at his neighbors—all of them armed. "So? Besides, that was their choice to play covert operatives." Closest to them were Gretchen and Ethel, who sat together with Ethel's husbands, Patrick and Sam. The Stone brothers sat in the booth closest to the entry door with Amber. The Knights were on the opposite side of the aisle with their new lady, Megan. There were other gun-toting citizens in Lucy's ready to act. Phoebe Blue sat at a table with her older brother, Corey, a US Marshal. Outside, too, were more neighbors on guard. Leading the self-proclaimed posse was Dylan, Jason, and Alexei. "You gotta love this town, Chicago. We do come together to protect our own."

Suddenly, she smiled. "That's for sure." Just as fast her lips thinned into a frown. "But none of this would've happened to Destiny if it hadn't been for me coming here."

"Stop being so hard on yourself, Nicole." Sawyer put his arm around her. "We were already on the Mitrofanov's radar before you got here. You know about Amber. Sergei came looking for her, not you. You being here is a help, not a hindrance."

Nicole leaned her head into Sawyer's shoulder.

Reed was impressed by his brother's words. Sawyer knew just what to say and when to say it. "I thought we'd have Henry by now."

"Henry may not be the insider, Reed." Nicole repeated the mantra she would say anytime Henry's name came up in the conversation. "We don't know it's him."

Sometimes Reed wished he were more like Sawyer, knowing

when to talk and when to shut up. "What about you, Mr. Intuitive? What are your thoughts on the topic?"

Sawyer shrugged. "I've never met the guy. My talents usually depend on knowing someone or at least meeting them in person."

"Like you did with me?" Nicole asked. "You seemed to get me from the first moment we met."

Sawyer grabbed her hand. "Exactly like that, sweetheart. Henry is innocent until proven guilty in my book."

"What about your book, Reed?"

"Sure. Why not?"

Nicole huffed out her frustration and then began chewing on her luscious lower lip.

Reed took another bite, but no pop of flavor hit his taste buds. After swallowing the bland food, he reached over and cupped her chin. "Baby, who knows who is coming or even if anyone is coming. My vote is to pull the plug on this and get to work on finding your friend back in Chicago."

"Please. Let's give Alexei's plan another day," Nicole said. "I do have a favor to ask though."

"Anything," Reed said, knowing he would move mountains for her if need be.

"I've never missed a weekly meeting since my recovery started two years ago. I checked online before I came to Destiny to see if there was a local group session here. There is. It meets tomorrow. Do you know who runs it?"

Sawyer nodded. "Sam O'Leary. He runs several groups in town. He's married to Ethel."

"I thought her husband was Patrick. That's what she called him on the phone during the fire anyway."

"Patrick is Sam's brother. They are both married to her."

"Following the Destiny tradition I see." Once again, the woman who invaded every one of Reed's thought smiled. God, he would never tire of seeing her happy. Never.

"Patrick is the businessman. Sam is the psychologist. Neither of them can settle into retirement." Sawyer stood up. "Let me get him for you, sweetheart."

As his brother walked away, Reed grabbed Nicole's hand. "What makes you think you're an addict, Chicago? I've known a lot of addicts in my life and you just don't fit the bill."

"But I am, Reed." She squeezed his hands with her delicate fingers. "I don't deserve you and Sawyer. And you guys deserve better than an addict like me."

"Baby, you've got it turned around. Even though you deserve better than two cowboys like Sawyer and me, I'll be damned if I'll ever let you go now that we've found you. You're stuck with us, Chicago."

"Sounds like you're thinking something more permanent to me, cowboy. You always work so fast."

"Not until you, Nicole."

Sawyer returned with Sam by his side. Sam, like his brother Patrick, was a distinguished-looking man. Both were like grandfathers to him, Sawyer, Erica, and all the other orphans from the plane crash. Sam's bright blue eyes shined behind the lens of his John Lennon-looking glasses. Though bald, Sam wore a full silver beard. As usual, Sam's smile lit up the room. Reed looked over at Nicole, who was just as entranced by Sam as everyone else.

"Miss Flowers, I am so glad to finally get to meet you. Ethel has told me so much about you I feel like I already know you." Sam offered his hand to her, which she took gladly.

"Nice to meet you, too, Dr. O'Leary."

"Please, just call me Sam."

"If you call me Nicole, you have a deal."

"Done, Nicole. Sawyer said you were interested in attending a meeting I run."

"Yes. I looked on the Internet and it says there's a meeting tomorrow at nine."

"There is. We actually meet every day of the week over in my office at O'Leary Tower. We would love to have you. Coffee and donuts are served, too."

"I'll be there," she said.

"Excellent. Now, I better get back to my post before Dylan and Jason dock my pay for this stakeout," Sam said, smiling, and went back to his booth.

Sawyer sat back down. "How much longer before we move to the next locale?"

Nicole looked back at the iPad's screen. "Fifteen more minutes. What can we do to fill this time?"

"Fifteen minutes isn't long enough, but I have an idea what you might enjoy, Chicago." He touched the back of her hand, wishing again they were alone and back at the cabin.

"Hold your horses, cowboy. You know how I feel about our situation already, Reed."

"You're right, baby. It is *our* situation, and you know how I feel, too."

"Have I missed something?" Sawyer asked.

"Chicago thinks she's not good enough for us. Can you believe that shit, bro?"

Sawyer shook his head. "I wish you could see yourself like we do, sweetheart. It doesn't matter if you were an addict or not. The past is the past. This is the here and now."

"And the future," Reed added, hoping to get Nicole to warm up to them.

"There's also another issue," she said in a very firm tone. "What about your lifestyle, guys?"

"We've already gone over that, Nicole." Sawyer brushed the hair out of her eyes. "Whatever you need us to be, we'll be that for you. BDSM or vanilla. All that matters is for us to be together. We've got something here. Something special. Can you deny that?"

She shook her head, and then fixed her gaze on Reed. "But is that enough for both of you?"

Reed wanted to tell her what Sawyer had just said. Whatever she needed him to be, he would be. But could he? Being a great Dom was something he'd always prided himself in. But could he be that with Nicole? He wasn't sure. Detachment from emotions helped him in the life. Hell, helped his life, helped him live. Feelings had nearly crushed him after his parents' death. Now, he was open to letting them in for *her*. For Nicole. For the woman he wanted to spend the rest of his life with. But BDSM? He couldn't see how that would fit with her, but even more how it would fit with him being a slave to his feelings for her. He couldn't be good at dominance, not really. Vanilla wasn't ideal for Reed, but for her, he would embrace generic with both hands. Time to convince her.

"Chicago, do you know what went through my head when the floor collapsed at the fire?"

She shook her head, and he saw her eyes water.

"You. Only you. I've never felt like this before, baby. I've never wanted anyone as much as I want you."

Nicole closed her eyes. "Me either."

"Forget your old life. Let it go. You, me, and Sawyer can embrace *our* new life. Together."

"I want to, Reed." She turned to Sawyer. "I do. You both are amazing and wonderful. So different in many ways but in the ones that matter the most—like kindness, honesty, warmth—the same. You keep talking about a future with me. Maybe there is a way to get there, but this is all so fast. Too fast, really. And I can't even think about that right now until I find Henry. Can you understand that?"

He and Sawyer each grabbed one of her hands. "Yes, Chicago. I understand and I know Sawyer does, too."

"I do," Sawyer said. "This is fast, sweetheart. You have a heavy load. We'll be patient with you. I promise."

"We also promise that when this is all over, me and my brother are going to win you. Trust me."

"I want to," she said, smiling weakly. She looked down at the iPad. "Time to go. Back to Alexei's schedule." '

The bell on the entry door to Lucy's chimed. A man walked in. A man in a Chicago police officer's uniform. He and Sawyer leapt from the booth, placing themselves between Nicole and the intruder. Like everyone else in Lucy's, their guns were out and pointed at the man.

Was he the dirty cop that Alexei's elaborate trap had been set for? God, Reed hoped so.

If the insider had taken the bait of the bad information Alexei had sent up to Nicole's station—and that was a very big "if"—the insider was likely in town looking for an opportunity to get to her. Traipsing the woman he was in love with around town to lure out the villain wasn't something he wanted to continue to do.

"What the hell is going on?" the guy barked.

"Best to put your hands up, fellow," Sam said.

The man's face stormed with shock and fire, but he wasn't a fool, sending his arms over his head.

"Let me see," Nicole said, coming out of the booth in a single bound.

"Chicago, you can look but no closer than by my side," Reed ordered.

When she saw the man, her eyes widened. "Jaris?"

Chapter Seventeen

Nicole couldn't believe Jaris was in Destiny. "What are you doing here?"

"What do you think this creep came to our town for, Nicole?" Reed snapped. "He's the rat we've trapped."

"What kind of place is this?" Jaris looked around the room of customers, each pointing their weapons at him. It took her back to the secret he'd kept for her when she had—while high on patrol—almost shot him.

"For you, young man, think of it as your last stop," Gretchen said, holding a fifty-caliber Smith & Wesson handgun. "Best not to move or you'll be looking more like Swiss cheese than a person."

"Can't you people see I'm a cop?" Jaris kept his hands above his head.

"Everyone stop this. Please," she said, as her mind went back to that alley where they'd been chasing a mugger.

"Nicole, I'll go around the building and cut him off," Jaris said. "You keep going."

Her mind was fuzzy. Another night without sleep, spent caring for Granddad, had taken so much out of her. She'd popped an additional two pills to try to get some rest. She was still groggy this morning from the effects. She needed coffee.

Nicole headed down the alley, trying hard to focus. A man jumped in front of her. She pointed her gun at his chest. If anyone was going to die today, it wasn't going to be her.

"Nicole," a familiar voice said. "It's me, Nicole. It's Jaris."

His face came into view and her hands began to shake. She'd almost killed her partner.

Jaris never told anyone of her mistake.

Entering the restaurant from outside, Dylan, Jason, and Alexei came in behind Jaris, pulling her back from her thoughts.

"Henry, put your hands behind your back," the sheriff ordered, holding a pair of cuffs in one hand and his revolver in the other.

"He's not Henry, Sheriff," Nicole told him. How could Jaris be the insider for the Mitrofanov's? It just didn't make any sense. But here he was. In Destiny.

"Who are you?" Dylan asked.

"I'm Jaris Simmons. I'm a cop, for chrissakes. What's this all about, Nicole?"

"Don't talk to her, asshole. Don't even fucking look at her," Sawyer's rage clearly was boiling inside him apparently fueled by his desire to protect her. But she didn't need protecting, at least not from Jaris. Or did she?

"Sawyer, stop. I know him. He's my old partner. Let us talk."

"Fine, baby. Talk. But no closer. You stay here and that asshole can stay there."

"You got a deal. Thanks." She turned to Jaris, the man who had pulled her out of the proverbial gutter on more than one occasion. "What are you doing here?"

Jason cuffed his hands behind his back while all of Lucy's customers put away their respective guns except Reed and Sawyer. Their weapons remained locked in on Jaris.

"Henry is missing."

"I know. How did you know where I was?"

"He told me the day you left. Said you were working on something dangerous."

"And?"

"And Henry said he had contacted the sheriff here to keep an eye on you in case things got out of hand."

"You still haven't answered my question, Jaris. Why are you here?"

"I came here for you, Nicole. When Henry didn't show up at the station without so much as a word, I went to his place. No Henry."

"You working alone, Simmons, or are there other of Mitrofanov's men in my town with you?" Jason asked.

"Mitrofanov?" Jaris looked her in the eyes. "Is that what you're working on, Nicole? Damn it, do you know how dangerous that is?"

"Quite the actor, Simmons. Academy-Award-winning performance, if you to be asking me," Alexei said.

"Sheriff, can we take this to your office? There's something you need to know."

"Everyone in here is deputized, Simmons."

"Everyone?"

"Yep. So whatever you have to say to me, you can say right here in front of these good people."

"It's sensitive information."

"Spill it, mister," Ethel said. "I'm the county judge in Swanson and you're wearing my patience thin. You don't want to piss me off."

"Jaris, please," Nicole said, still in shock to see her friend here in Destiny. "Do you know where Henry is or not?"

"I don't, Nicole, but I am working undercover with the FBI. Or at least I was before I got to this town." Jaris shook his head. "They recruited me to help smoke out the mole in the station. I've been on the job with them for over a year now."

"Easy to check out," Dylan told Jason. "I'll make some phone calls. I can have the facts by tomorrow at the latest."

"Until then, Simmons, you'll be enjoying the comforts of the Swanson County Jail. Come with me."

"I'm going with him," Nicole said.

"The hell you are." Reed blocked her from moving closer.

"He's my partner. Don't try to stop me, cowboy."

As Jason led Jaris out of Lucy's, Reed cupped her chin. "I won't *try*. I will stop you."

A shiver ran up and down her spine. "I'm a cop. When will you two get it through your thick heads I can take care of myself?"

His tone softened slightly, warming her insides. "Now that we're here you don't have to, Chicago."

"What if he's telling the truth?" she asked, hearing her voice come out so small it surprised her.

"If his story pans out, then you can talk to him but not until." He kissed her on the forehead.

She wanted to argue with the maverick giant in front of her, but couldn't seem to find the words. Something about his change in demeanor had a powerful impact on her. She felt tiny, feminine, and protected. The truth was she liked how he made her feel right now. Was this his Dom side showing? If it was, she definitely wanted to see more of it.

"Where to until Dylan gets back with us?" Sawyer asked.

"Our cabin," Reed said.

Our cabin. Nicole loved the sound of that.

Chapter Eighteen

Still reeling from the knowledge that Jaris might actually be the insider and the one responsible for Henry's disappearance, Nicole followed Sawyer and Reed into the cabin that had been a kind of sanctuary for her from the life she'd left behind a few days ago. Still, her past had followed her here to Destiny somehow.

After placing his Stetson on the hat rack by the front door, Reed stepped right in front of her, his eyes full of sympathy. "Baby, would you like us to get a bath ready for you? It might help take your mind off of all this shit."

"Nothing is going to be able to do that." *Henry? Where are you?* She collapsed on the sofa and brought her hands to her face. If Jaris was a dirty cop, then she couldn't be certain about anything anymore. Her judgment was worthless. "I can't believe this is happening." This was one of the lowest points in her life, and she'd had more than her fair share of them. Jaris had helped pull her out of one of the worst.

"Chicago, look at me."

She felt Reed's fingers in her hair, stroking gently. "I can't. This is too much. I can't handle this."

"Bullshit. Now, open your eyes and look at me."

She blinked and Reed's face came into focus.

He smiled. "Good. Your mind is buzzing like a fallen beehive."

She was exhausted and finding it hard to hold back the damn tears that were stinging her eyes. Her world had been turned upside down, twisted, and shredded. Nothing made sense anymore. "So? Can you blame me? Henry is gone, maybe dead. A man who I've known since my rookie days might be a criminal. I came to Destiny to try to do some real police work because of a missing persons report with my name on it. I thought I could fix everything. Clear Henry's name. Get my old job back. Bring down the Russians. What did I do? I fucked up everything. I brought hell to Destiny. I–I...I can't..." The dam broke and the salty tears streamed down her cheeks.

Reed kissed her eyes closed. "Shh. You're trying to make sense out of something that can't be sorted out tonight. Not by you. Not by us. Not by anyone. Dylan is the man to get to the bottom of things. That means tomorrow we'll have the facts of whether Jaris is telling the truth or lying."

She opened her eyes and looked from Reed to Sawyer and back again. "Jaris is a friend. A real friend. You don't know what he's done for me."

Both of their faces seemed to harden as their lips thinned and their eyes narrowed. Had she said something to anger them? What?

She ventured to find out. "What's going on in your heads?"

"Do you love this Jaris fellow?" Sawyer's razor-sharp tone made her shiver. Jealousy? A terrifying sight on him.

"As a friend only. A dear friend, but that's all. We've never thought of each other that way. He's like a brother to me, I swear."

Sawyer smiled his approval.

Reed nodded, letting out a big gust of air between his thick, manly lips. "You need a distraction, Chicago."

"My brother is right about that," Sawyer chimed in.

"Nothing can distract me tonight, guys. I doubt I'll sleep a single wink until I know the truth about my partner and about Henry."

"Is that a challenge, sweetheart?" Sawyer asked.

"No." Somewhere deep inside her seemed to stir to his salacious undercurrent.

"Sounded like a challenge to me," he said. "What did it sound like to you, Reed?"

"Definitely a challenge." His voice deepened to a timbre that vibrated her skin. God, the man was beautiful. Too beautiful. Reed moved forward until the only thing between them was their clothing, just thin layers of fabric. Tiny woven threads were the only things separating her skin from his. Her nipples tightened as she felt Sawyer come up behind her just as close as Reed was in her front.

"Guys, we should wait to hear from Dylan. What if he gets news earlier?" The logical thing was to hold back. The slippery slope they were offering her would send her crashing into certain heartbreak. She needed to avoid going down this delicious path with them again, no matter how pleasurable it might be. *Logic. Be logical, Nicole.* No matter how much she tried to hold on to that idea, she kept picturing them making love to her the other night. As if they had minds of their own, her hands shot up to Reed's shoulders, curling around his thick muscles there.

"No cell service here, baby." Sawyer kissed the back of her neck. "Remember that? Whatever Dylan discovers about Jaris will hold until morning."

Tomorrow would come and she would finally know the truth about her former partner. Whatever the outcome, she needed to leave Destiny. Her throat tightened as her cowboys squeezed her body between them.

The little town and its wonderful, eccentric people had changed her. They'd taken up arms to protect her. God, it would be hard to say good-bye. Even harder would be to never see Reed and Sawyer again. But Reed was still holding some of himself back from her. BDSM mattered to him. That was clear to her. He seemed not to trust she would be able to handle it. Maybe he was right. And though Sawyer was ready and open, there was no way she would break up these brothers. Never.

She opened her mouth to tell them to take her back to town when Reed pressed his mouth to hers. She felt his tongue trace the line of her lips, and all her hesitation, her logic vanished. All that remained was desire—desire to be taken, to be touched, to be held and consumed by her two cowboys.

Reed's kiss went deeper and deeper, like a claim on her heart that would never be lifted. Her legs softened and fresh quivers rolled through her.

When he released her lips, he lifted her up into his arms as if she was made of helium.

He and Sawyer took her to the bedroom and gently placed her on the mattress.

Reed covered her with his body, his weight securing her to the bed and to him. His muscled chest pressed against her breasts, causing her nipples to tighten. Even dressed, she could feel his cock through all the fabric between them on her pussy. As he used his legs to spread her legs wider, a hot tingle vibrated in her center, spreading out from her belly to her pussy and down her thighs. Now, his cock felt even closer.

Reed brought his mouth to hers, and again, she melted into his lusty, seductive lips. All her doubts and worries scurried to the back of her mind and her instincts took charge, her feminine instincts. Reed and Sawyer were everything Nicole had ever wanted or needed. She wanted to be theirs, to surrender all of herself to them—to be what they needed her to be.

She moaned into Reed's hot kiss, her toes curling and her fingers tugging at his hair.

Suddenly, their kiss ended and Reed's weight came off her body. As Reed left the mattress, she watched Sawyer, devoid of all his clothes, move onto the bed next to her. Glancing down between his legs she saw his monstrous, erect cock.

Why did she feel so good with Sawyer and Reed? Why did her dark existence vanish just being around them? Because she could be herself and let go, let go of all the doubt and worry.

"Beautiful." Sawyer gazed at her with the most loving eyes she'd ever seen.

He kissed her, causing her heart to swell and her body to warm.

Never releasing his mouth from hers, Sawyer skillfully removed her clothing. How? She wasn't sure, but it took him only seconds to free her of every thread. As he moved his lips off her mouth to her neck, she felt a growing pressure between her legs. She was wet and warm. A thirst to feel the friction of his body on hers shook her to the core. No way could she remain still when every shred of her body screamed to be touched. As Sawyer shifted from her side to cover her with his naked frame, she clawed at his chest.

Sawyer slipped to her right side.

Reed, now as naked as she and Sawyer, crawled next to her on her left. "Your tits are gorgeous, Chicago." His big hand covered her left breast. "Have you ever seen any like hers, Sawyer?"

Sawyer started massaging her right breast. "No way. These are female perfection." His thumb flicked over her nipple again and again, increasing the tingle and ache in them with each pass.

Reed traced his fingers over her lips, which were swollen and throbbing from all the kissing. "Nicole, you're...I've never thought..." He closed his eyes, clearly wrestling with something deep-seated within him.

God, his still waters ran deeper than hers. "Shh, cowboy."

"Fuck," he cursed, closing his eyes tight.

They both were damaged, him by the loss of his parents and her by the loss of her grandfather. She understood how hard it was to reach those buried emotions, to open up to someone. "I'm here. Right now, Reed. You're here. It'll keep for later." She prayed he would break through his walls. She needed him. Needed both of them. But Reed was the key to making it work. She knew that. If he couldn't let her into his secret life of BDSM, then what kind of future could they have? They couldn't have a future at all.

"Reed, you okay?" Sawyer asked, concern for his younger brother in every syllable.

"He's fine," Nicole said. These men had given her hope again. The least they deserved was for her to try to be what they needed her to be. She moved her hands up into Reed's silky blond hair. "Look at me, cowboy."

He opened his eyes and she could see the ancient pain he carried there.

"It'll keep." She tugged on his hair, an invitation for another kiss.

He bent down and devoured her lips like a man dying of thirst. She whimpered into his mouth, feeling her own past pain merge with his.

Please let me in, Reed. Let me in. I need you as much as you need me.

Sawyer swallowed her nipple, flicking his tongue against her taut bit of flesh. Every cell in her fired for more.

As Reed's tongue swept through her mouth and Sawyer's bathed her breast, circles of heat grew inside her—one from each intimate kiss. The circles spun and blazed and then shot down her body and straight into her pussy, causing her clit to throb.

Reed ended their kiss and went to work on her other nipple. He scraped his teeth over her throbbing bits, making her squirm and moan.

"God, your lust smells good, Nicole." Sawyer's forceful talk was working her into a frantic bundle of need. "I think I'll take a sip of her cream right now." He ran his hands down her abdomen to just within striking distance of her clit.

"Please touch me," Nicole panted, her need so intense she could no longer hold back.

Reed laved her nipple into a peak of aching desire. The rumble in his throat was more animal than human to her ear. Hunger and danger resided deep inside the man and she wanted him and Sawyer to consume all of her.

"Spread your legs wide for me, baby," Sawyer ordered, his thumb circling her clit but never touching. She was mad for him to at least graze the bud and relieve some of the extreme pressure building inside.

She moved her legs far apart from one another as he'd

commanded.

"That's what I like to see from you, sweetheart. Surrender." Sawyer's thumb pressed on her clit and her pussy clenched and her back came off the mattress. He removed it and the pressure came back with more fury.

Reed's teeth captured her throbbing nipple and clamped down slightly, creating a sweet bite of pleasure that mushroomed into a swirl of need that shot straight down to her pussy.

Sawyer shifted down until his head was between her thighs. Using his fingers, he threaded her folds, parting her pussy's lips. She could feel his hot breath on her most intimate flesh and it added to the increasing strain for relief inside her. When his tongue flicked her clit, a delicious dizziness spun her around.

"That's it, baby. Give me your sweet cream." Sawyer kissed her clit, his lips delivering a light tap that raised the pressure and increased her trembles. His thick tongue slid over her folds, creating a friction that seemed to envelop not only her pussy, but her whole being. Her skin tingled. Her pulse raced. Her breathing became shallow.

Reed's manic kissing of her breasts and Sawyer's wandering fingertips on her pussy were working to send her over the edge.

"God, you taste so good, Nicole." Sawyer continued drinking from her pussy, making her hotter and more needy than she'd ever felt before.

"Please. I need you." *Please, Reed, open up. Show me your Dom side.*

"That you do, baby," Sawyer said. "That you do." He shifted slightly away from her for a moment, getting something from the table by the bed. When he shifted back, she saw the condom packages in his hand and the bottle of lube. "Reed, here."

Reed barely acknowledged him, but took the foil package from Sawyer.

"Baby, you're going to enjoy this, I promise. Have you ever had anal sex before?"

She shook her head. The truth was she'd never even considered it would be something she would try before. *I can do this. For Sawyer. For Reed.*

"Time to flip our lovely cop over, Reed. We need to get her ready to take you back there, okay?"

"Yes." The word came out more like a growl than anything else. Reed was clearly on his own edge, an edge she wanted him to get past.

Together they turned her whole body until she was facedown on the bed.

"Baby, we're going to take our time here." Sawyer's tone took on a confident, commanding note that she loved. "You've never had anal sex before so I want to make sure you're ready.

"The pleasure will be mind-blowing for you. I know what I'm doing," Reed whispered in her ear.

"Reed, you do it," Sawyer said. "You get her ass ready for you cock."

The ever-intuitive Sawyer clearly was sensing what she was in Reed. His walls were up. Why? Fear. Fear of what? She wasn't sure, but Sawyer was trying to push him past them.

She heard the pop of the lid of the bottle of lubricant and then the squirting noise of its liquid being released. Her body was on fire, her pussy clenching tighter and tighter as the pressure continued to rise inside her. She felt Reed's hands on her ass. He spread her cheeks and moved his thick, long fingertips to her tight entrance, slicking it up with lube.

"Breathe, Chicago," Reed said, sounding more in control of himself than before.

She obeyed him instantly and felt him pierce her ass with one finger. The sting was quick but faded as Sawyer pressed on her clit with the tips of his fingers from one hand and splayed out her pussy's lips with the ones from his other hand. Reed stretched her anus and sent in another finger. And again, Sawyer worked on her throbbing clitoris and soaked pussy turning the bite of Reed's intruding fingers into heavy need. Over and over, these brothers worked their magic on her pussy and ass until she was gasping and thrashing on the bed, biting the sheets as the pressure inside her multiplied.

"She's ready, Reed. Time to give Nicole her first double penetration."

"Yes. God, yes. Please." She'd never begged for anything, let alone during sex, but there was no holding back what she needed from them. "Fill me. I have to have you inside me. Both of you."

"The sweetest pleading from the prettiest lips I've ever seen," Sawyer said. "Let's get her off the bed and into our arms between us, Reed."

Sawyer lifted her up off the bed. "Hold on to me, baby." She could feel his cock against her pussy.

She wrapped her legs around his waist and her arms around his neck.

"That's perfect. I've got you." Sawyer was taking charge. She loved hearing the command in his tone.

Reed came up behind her and she wondered how his Dom voice would sound. His thick cock pressed between her ass cheeks. "Chicago, don't worry. I know what I'm doing. Trust me."

"I do." *With all my heart, Reed.*

"I'll go slow at first." Reed sent the big, bulbous head of his cock past her ass's tight ring. At first the burn was too hot, the sting too intense, but Sawyer skillfully shifted his hips so that his cock pressed against her clit just right, driving her mad and creating delicious sensations in her entire body. "That's it, Chicago. Take me in."

With his big hands on the back of her thighs, Reed sent his thick dick deeper into her ass, filling and stretching her back there. Every fraction of an inch he took sent a wave of new sensations through her body. Once Reed's cock was fully seated in her ass, she sighed into Sawyer's chest—the place that held his strong and loving heart.

The sting she'd felt the moment Reed had pierced her ass was gone, leaving her with a hungry burn for more. She'd never wanted like this before in her whole life.

She didn't deserve them, but they thought she did.

Reed groaned behind her, and she felt him begin thrusting into her ass in long steady strokes, each pressing her harder into Sawyer's frame.

"You okay, Nicole?"

"Uh-huh," was the only response she could get out, lost in the overwhelming sensations of having Reed's cock fill her from behind. More moan-like than words, but Nicole hoped he understood she loved every bit of this. Let tomorrow be whatever, right now she was here squeezed between two men who had captured her heart.

"I know, baby. I know." Of course Sawyer could understand her. She'd never had a chance of keeping anything from the sexy, mind-reading cowboy. "Time for me to feel your tight, pretty pussy on my dick."

Another moan, less articulate that the last, but Sawyer's eyes told her he knew how much she wanted him inside her.

He shifted his hips again until the head of his cock was on the lips of her pussy. With the help of Reed, whose hands were on the back of her thighs, Sawyer lowered her down slowly onto his massive, thick cock.

As he filled up her pussy, she scraped at his shoulders with her fingernails. *I have them both inside my body. I'm theirs and they are mine.*

"Breathe, Chicago," Reed whispered in her ear. "You're holding your breath. Don't."

She hadn't even realized it, lost to the sensations they'd created in her. She inhaled as deep as she could at the moment, which turned out to be a half breath.

As her cowboys began synchronizing the thrusts of their cocks into her body, her half breaths divided into quarters and then into eighths until she was panting between their muscled bodies like a wild woman. Never had she felt so taken, so full, so claimed. As a powerful undulation shot through all the pressure that had built up, she was able to take a giant breath into her lungs, which immediately shot back up her throat and out her mouth into a scream of release. Sensations so powerful and unimaginable swamped her utterly. As her orgasm swelled again and again, she thrashed between the cowboys who'd stolen her heart. They would never give it back and she would never take it from them.

She tightened her lower half, using her pussy and ass to clamp down on her cowboys' cocks.

"Fuuuck." Reed's body slammed into her as he sent his cock into her ass one final time.

Sawyer's eyes closed and she felt his cock pulse against the walls of her sex as he came inside her. After a long, sweaty pause, Sawyer and Reed carried her back to the bed, returning to the positions they'd had earlier, one on each side of her.

Even though she'd told them about her dark past, they still wanted her, really wanted. More than that even. Reed and Sawyer had made it quite clear they had chosen her. They would not back down until she accepted their offer of a new life. Maybe she did deserve them after all. The more they told Nicole she did deserve them, the more she was beginning to believe it herself. But she wouldn't settle for only half of Reed. No. That wouldn't be fair to him or to her.

She'd never been so close, so exposed, so open to anyone like she was with Sawyer and Reed. This felt right. This was where she belonged. Sawyer held back nothing. All his chips were on the line. Nicole wanted to prove to Reed she could be the woman he really needed. Whatever their lifestyle held, she would jump in with both feet gladly. How could she make Reed understand that?

"Spank me, Reed. I want to feel your hand on my ass."

His lips pressed on hers, silencing her request and breaking her heart. "Not now, Chicago."

"Letting a sub top you from the bottom, bro. That's not like you."

Reed didn't answer him. "Sweetheart, you've been distracted enough for tonight. Go to sleep. We've got a lot to face tomorrow morning when we get up."

Nicole nodded, despite feeling her dream of a future with them fall completely apart. Reed's "not now" really meant "not ever" and "not with me." Why wouldn't he let her see his Dom side? He didn't trust her with BDSM, which was a big part of his life, his makeup.

Instead of turning to Sawyer to try to get a read on what he thought about Reed's statement, Nicole closed her eyes. Did it matter what she or Sawyer thought now? Though never discussing it aloud, they'd silently agreed during their lovemaking through quick glances and hurried winks to try to push Reed to open up to her. It hadn't worked.

"Everything is going to be okay, baby." Sawyer kissed her on the cheek. "You'll see."

Nicole wanted to look at both of them, really look at them to create a lasting image she could call up whenever she wanted. But she didn't. Instead she kept her eyes shut. "Good night, guys," she said in the steadiest tone she could muster.

"Good night, Chicago."

"Good night, baby."

How long she stayed between them with her eyes closed forcing her tears into submission she didn't know. It felt like back-to-back eternities. When Reed and Sawyer's breathing changed to a rhythm that let her know they'd fallen asleep, Nicole let the tears fall. She would never find love again, of that she was certain. Even though her heart seized a tiny bit at the thought of another being held by them, Nicole truly hoped they would find a future with someone special. They deserved to be happy.

Chapter Nineteen

Sawyer sat next to Nicole in the sheriff's office holding her hand and sensing he and Reed were already losing her.

He looked over at Reed, who was staring out the window. What a fucked-up mess. Both Nicole and Reed had come so close last night to getting real with each other. How the hell was he going to get them to see that the three of them belonged together?

Shannon, the sheriff's dispatcher, opened the door wearing a bright pale-green wig. Colorful hairpieces had always been her signature statement. "Dylan just drove up, Jason. That Alexei guy is with him."

"Thanks," the sheriff said from his seat behind his big desk. "Send them right in."

Shannon nodded and went back to her desk in the other room.

Nicole seemed to be staring at the painting on the wall behind Jason, but Sawyer knew better. Her pupils weren't tight enough to focus on the landscape depicted inside its frame. She was terrified about what they were going to learn about her former partner, Jaris. The guy was still in a cell awaiting the verdict.

Dylan and Alexei came in.

Nicole stood and Sawyer spotted her hands trembling by her sides. "Don't leave us hanging. What did you two find out?"

"Jaris is legit," Dylan said from behind his ever-present sunglasses. "His story checks out. Jaris is an undercover operative with the FBI."

"Thank God." Nicole breathed out and returned to her chair.

Sawyer put his arm around her shoulders. "You were right, baby."

She nodded. "What about Henry? Did you find him?"

Dylan shook his head.

Alexei shrugged. "I do have news, too. Not good, I'm afraid. Niklaus Mitrofanov visit someone I believe the sheriff is familiar with. A Mr. Kip Lunceford."

"Who is Lunceford?" Nicole asked.

"He's a demented sonofabitch but he is also a brilliant bastard." Jason sighed. "You've met Megan. Kip Lunceford is her ex. He's also a serial killer who is locked up in a maximum-security prison. How the hell did Mitrofanov get access to Kip, Alexei?"

"Niklaus got favor from some major players in Chicago," the former Russian mobster said. "Bad idea for him. Better to be a loaner of debts than a taker of them."

The sheriff frowned. "Sounds like you care about this fucker's success too much."

Alexei shook his head. "No. I just know ropes of organization. They are very tricky things to be tying. Niklaus will have high interest to pay one day to The Outfit, mark my words."

Reed's eyebrows rose. "The Outfit?"

"The Chicago mob is known by that name," Nicole informed. "What favor, Alexei?"

"The visit," the big man continued. "It happened with blessing of some dirty politician. I don't to be finding out name yet, but I will."

"You think this Kip fellow might have Henry stashed somewhere?" Nicole asked.

"I can't see how since he's locked up." Jason's face was twisted into a knot of concern.

Nicole wrung her hands on her lap. "Could Lunceford be involved in Henry's disappearance somehow?"

Sawyer hated hearing the dread in her voice as she grasped at straws.

"I don't know. Maybe," Jason answered. "I just don't see what reason these two would have to join forces. To what end?"

"Revenge," Dylan answered. "Niklaus hates Destiny and its citizens for killing his son. Kip hates the Knights and has a horrible fascination for his ex-wife, Megan, their new love. They're both seeking the same thing. To destroy us."

"What else do you have for me?" Nicole asked, the harsh tone he'd heard from her back in her voice.

"This is all I have for now," Alexei said. "I am not through with my diggings though."

"Well get a bigger shovel then. I agreed to your plan because I thought it would help me find my friend. It didn't. My friend is still missing. I'm no closer to finding Henry than I was yesterday when Sheriff Wolfe put my other friend in cuffs and locked him up in a cell." Nicole turned to Jason and glared at him. "Don't you think it's time to release Jaris?"

"Okay. I'll get him." Jason got up and headed out his door. The jail was part of this building but sat in the back through another door to the right of the sheriff's office. Six cells. Sawyer had spent a night in one of them a year after his parents' deaths. He'd downed half a bottle of tequila and then gotten into a fight with some guys from Clover.

When Jason returned with Jaris, Nicole jumped up and put her arms around him, filling Sawyer with a big dose of the green-eyed monster. Sure she'd said she wasn't interested, but what about her old partner? How did he feel about her?

Nicole stepped back. "I'm so sorry, Jaris. This is all my fault."

"Why? You didn't put me in a cell." He pointed to Jason. "He did. Nicky, you've got to stop beating yourself up about everything. Sometimes shit just happens."

Sawyer's instincts backed down his resentment of Jaris. Her old partner clearly looked at Nicole as a little sister more than anything romantically. Also, Jaris wasn't trying to pull her into him in another embrace, to make all the other dick-swinging guys in the office know she was his. Of course, that was what Sawyer wanted to do right about now. Pull Nicole into his lap away from Jaris no matter his seemingly good intentions. Sawyer didn't, of course, knowing Nicole's current state. He had to keep his cool. Winning her heart had been the easiest part. The difficult part would be to earn her trust. Sawyer looked at Reed, who was calm on the outside but clearly a wreck on the inside. "Difficult" didn't even begin to describe the task in front of him.

"I'm going to Chicago to find Henry," she said.

"Not without me and Sawyer, you don't," Reed growled.

Nicole addressed Dylan, Alexei, and Jason. "Gentlemen, do you mind giving us a moment?"

The three left the room.

Nicole sighed. "I think it would best for us to part friends, don't you?"

"Hell no, I don't." Reed stepped up to her. "What's wrong, Chicago?"

God, how dense could his brother be? He wanted to scream at him. If Reed didn't wake up right now and tell her what was holding him back, they were going to lose Nicole, the woman of their dreams.

She turned to Jaris. "Will you help me find Henry?"

The cop nodded and a new wave of jealousy blasted Sawyer's insides. "Do you mind if we get some breakfast first, Nicky? I'm starving. The sheriff told me about the diner a block away from here. Blue's, I think he called it. I'd love some bacon and eggs."

"Sounds great." Nicole's walls were obviously up and intact again.

"We need to have Dylan set up a detail first," Reed said.

"I've already told you I'm done here. No detail. No bodyguards. No one. Jaris isn't just a cop as it turns out. I was right. I'm also right about Henry. He's in trouble. I know it in my bones. Jaris is FBI. Counting me, that makes two law enforcement officers that can take care of any mobster who might show up at our breakfast." She shook her head and closed her eyes tight. "But no one is coming. I've wasted time here in Destiny when I should've already been looking for Henry."

"Like it or not, Chicago, we are going with you to Illinois if that's where you're going." Reed might be coming around but was it too late? Still, Sawyer wasn't about to give up on having a life with Nicole and apparently neither was his brother.

"I'm so grateful to you both. Thank you for everything." She blinked several times but not a single tear fell.

Knowing she was shoving her emotions down crushed Sawyer. It wasn't just that he wanted her—God, knew he did. It was that she needed them. And he and Reed needed her, too.

There wasn't a day that Sawyer didn't think about his parents. Grief was part of him, too, but he'd learned long ago how to live through it and embrace life. His brother hadn't. All Reed's bravado and lustiness was just another kind of defense to keep himself locked away from the world. When Nicole had arrived he saw something in his brother he'd never seen before. Hope. But the woman who'd wrapped herself around their hearts had her own suffering. She didn't see her own value. *Value?* Fuck, she was priceless, a precious light that chased away the darkness inside his lonely world. In his heart, Sawyer knew that she was the only one for him and Reed.

The only one.

Nicole let out a long sigh. "I'd like to be alone with my friend of many years, a man who I knew in my heart was trustworthy."

"Thanks, Nicky. I trust you, too," Jaris said.

"We don't give a fuck what you think, Simmons," Reed snapped. "I won't leave you alone with Nicole. Not now. Not ever."

Nicole shook head. "God, you're killing me, Reed. Why can't you trust me?"

"I do trust you, Chicago. It's him I don't trust."

"You don't trust me. I know Jaris. I've known him much longer than I've known you. A lifetime compared to our time together."

"Baby, you—"

"Don't. It's too hard. All of this is too hard. It's also not fair to me. I want to talk to my friend alone. Can you give me that?"

"Yes," Reed said reluctantly. "Just breakfast. Sawyer and I will be right behind you and then we'll sit at another table."

"Dylan's proof is clear. It's safe for me to be with Jaris." She folded her arms over her chest. Sawyer could almost feel her heartache as she was plainly pulling away from them. His own heart was ripping apart. "I want you to stop trying to protect me."

"Have I missed something?" Jaris asked, glancing back and forth from Sawyer and Reed. Then he looked at Nicole. "If I were in these guys' position, I would feel the same way, Nicky. Why not let them come with us?"

"Because I don't want them to." Her words were like a knife to Sawyer's heart and by the look on Reed's face, they were to him, too.

Sawyer loved his brother and loved Nicole. They shared a bond that could heal their pulverizing pain. Somehow he had to find a way for them to open up their hearts, really open them up, to see how much they all needed each other.

She looked back and forth from him and Reed. "You've done so much for me. I'll never forget you. I promise. But it's time for me to go."

"Don't push us away. We're going to Chicago with you." Reed's rage boiled to the surface. Was he finally realizing what was going to happen if he didn't change course with Nicole?

"I wish you wouldn't, but if I can't stop you then I guess I can't. Do what you must."

"I don't understand," Reed said, the confusion evident on his face.

"That's the problem, cowboy." Nicole sighed. "Because I do understand." Then she left the sheriff's office with Jaris.

As the door slammed shut between Sawyer and the woman of his dreams, he realized she wasn't just headed to Blue's Diner for a private meal with her former partner. She was headed for Chicago and for a life without him and Reed.

* * * *

"What the fuck just happened?" Reed marched to the door. No way was he letting Nicole go without him.

"Wait," Sawyer said.

"I'm not waiting and leaving her with that fucking partner of hers." He felt every muscle tighten in his body.

Sawyer nodded. "Me either, but you and I need to talk for a second. Then we can head out. We're only steps away from her right now. If anything happens, which I strongly doubt, she and Jaris can handle it until we get there."

"She's in danger, bro. Have you forgotten about the insider?"

"Of course not. Give me a sec."

"The insider may not be Jaris, but that means Henry is the only suspect we have left. And we don't know where he is." Reed hated seeing Nicole leave. When that door had closed, it was like losing his parents all over again. He couldn't let that happen. Not with *her*.

"That's just it, Reed. We need to trust Nicole. She was right about Jaris. She's probably right about Henry, too."

"Then who is it?"

Sawyer shrugged. "We'll find out. We are going to Chicago. The Stones will give us the time off. They understand love's price."

"Yes, they do." Reed thought about Amber and how much she'd changed the Stone brothers' lives just like Nicole had for him.

Sawyer's eyes narrowed. "Do you understand love's price?"

Love's price? "What do you mean by that?"

"You think I don't see what Nicole sees. You're holding back, Reed. She asked you to spank her last night and you refused."

Reed's jaw tightened. "I didn't refuse. I knew we needed sleep."

"Don't bullshit me. I know you. Talk to me."

Sawyer and Erica were the only people he'd let himself trust and love after the crash. *Until Nicole.*

His brother deserved to know the ugly truth. "I just can't. I enjoyed training subs with you. I've always prided myself in being a great Dom. You know why? Because I kept myself detached. The scene was the important thing to me."

"You didn't care about the women we shared?"

"As sub students? Yes. More than that? No. I'm not sure I can be a good Dom with Nicole." *The truth. Tell him the truth.* "I love her. I've never loved anyone as much as I love her. How can I show Nicole the life if I can't control my emotions around her? I never thought I would choose a vanilla existence, but for her I will."

"What a fucking load of crap." Sawyer's face was hot. "Your choice isn't for her, Reed. It's for you."

"What the hell are you talking about?" He didn't like where this conversation was going. Not one fucking bit.

"She wants to try BDSM. She's told us that again and again and you've pushed her away."

He grabbed the doorknob, needing an escape from Sawyer, who was getting dangerously close to something he didn't want to face.

"Get a grip on yourself, Reed. And your new emotions. It's time for you to embrace your inner Dom."

"I can't, damn it." He'd never felt so raw, so exposed before. But he had to let it out, had to make Sawyer understand. "If I could, don't you think I would have already? Nicole matters to me. I can't be a Dom with her. You've got to see that, bro."

"You want to know how a real Dom feels? They feel so much it would crush most, but they care more for their sub than themselves. Goddamn it, Reed, be a Dom. You're a fucking selfish idiot and we're going to lose Nicole if you don't open up to her."

Lose Nicole? No way. He wasn't losing her. She was his. Theirs. The love of his life. Sawyer was right. He had been an idiot. Nicole had told him her darkest secret and deepest fear. And what had he done? Crawled back into his shell.

With all his heart Reed wanted a life, a future, a family with her and Sawyer.

Time to Dom up.

"Let's go get *our* Chicago."

* * * *

With her heart ripped to shreds, Nicole walked with Jaris out of the sheriff's office and onto the sidewalk that ran up and down East Street.

"Nicky, are you okay?" Jaris asked.

"No, but I don't want to talk about it."

"You love them, don't you? Those two cowboys back there."

She nodded, leading the way across East to go down the park side of North Street. "Crazy, huh?"

"Not a traditional life but not a crazy one either. The sheriff here isn't half bad. He brought me dinner last night. He filled me in on what sets Destiny apart from other places. Why not choose love? You've been through so much, Nicky. You deserve a chance at a better life, don't you?"

"Here? With Sawyer and Reed?" Coming to the base of the dragon statue on the northeast corner of the street, she glanced up and looked at the heart on the shield it held. "This is the Red Dragon. Did the sheriff tell you about the town's dragons?"

"He did. I think Wolfe needed a friendly ear, and apparently, even though I was his prisoner, he chose me. This dragon is about passion, right?"

"That's what I've been told. Reed and Sawyer and I spent a couple of days together just talking." She swallowed down her heartache. Her recovery from addiction had been hard. Her recovery from love? It would be hell, if it ever arrived at all. "Let's go. Since you seem so interested in Destiny, let me show you another dragon. It's just up the block between us and Blue's." She increased her pace, and Jaris kept up beside her.

"Nicky, listen to me. You deserve happiness. There's nothing for you in Chicago. Here, you can build a new life."

"It doesn't matter. It will never work out for me with Reed and Sawyer. Let's go eat and then we can get back to Chicago and looking for Henry."

"Nicky, you're doing it again."

"Doing what?"

"Being too hard on yourself."

"Old habits die hard, Jaris." She wanted to change the subject and refocus on the case. "Can you tell me about the missing persons report you gave me on Kathy White? Why did it have Sergei Mitrofanov's name listed as her husband?"

"Nicky, what are you talking about?" Suddenly, Jaris stopped. He seemed puzzled. "That report came from Patti. She asked me to give it to you."

Chapter Twenty

Right at the base of the Black Dragon, Nicole shook her head. "I can't believe that, Jaris. Patti? Our friend Patti?" But in her heart, she knew it had to be true.

"I guess you are as dumb as you look, slut." Patti came out from the other side of the statue but remained in the shadows a few feet from them. In her hand was a gun. She had a cigarette dangling from her mouth. "We've never been friends, but you've been too stupid to see that, haven't you?"

She's the insider. Patti's face was bright red. She was sweating profusely. It looked as if she was running a high fever. A tank top revealed deep scratches on her shoulder. They appeared to be full of infection.

Connie had given her that wound. *Oh my God! Patti was the shooter the other night. She's the insider.*

Nicole's heart thudded in her chest like a sledgehammer. "Why are you here, Patti?"

"Shut the fuck up, bitch. I'm not talking to you. Only to him." She pointed to Jaris, who was moving his hand slowly up to his gun, which the sheriff had returned to him.

"Don't even think about it, lover. Keep your hands down."

Jaris nodded. "Don't do anything you'll regret, Patti."

"Too late for that, babe." Patti glared at her. "I've been confined in another hellhole up the road from here. Clover, Colorado. Three days I've been sneaking in and out of this fucking place—undetected. Waiting for the perfect opportunity to do what I came here for. Patience finally paid off. Here the slut is, right in front of me."

"You're working with the Mitrofanovs," Jaris stated flatly.

"Great detective work, Jaris. You learn that from the FBI?"

Nicole knew it was a risk to push Patti, but she must. "Did you have anything to do with Henry's disappearance?"

"I won't tell you again, slut. Shut. The. Fuck. Up." Patti pointed the barrel of her gun right at Nicole.

"Then tell me, Patti," Jaris said in gentle tone. "What happened to Henry? What's going on with you? Talk to me. We're partners."

The hardness in Patti's face softened. "Yes, I know what happened to Henry. Jaris, everything I did, I did for us. When this bitch vanished from the station without telling me where she was going, I knew I was in trouble. Fuck, if you hadn't shown up two years ago, I wouldn't have to be dealing with her today."

"What about two years ago?" he asked quietly. Nicole's and his training was kicking in. Negotiation protocols with an assailant were clear. Keep them talking.

"Might as well put all my cards on the table. I don't have a chance of surviving more than a week with the Mitrofanov's hit on me." Patti snorted. "You know I hate coffee. Hate it with a passion. But I drank it so that I could get the slut to drop her guard. It worked. After she told me about her little slipup taking her granddad's pain meds to sleep, I knew drugging her would be simple. A little in her coffee every day. My plan was to get her drug tested and off the force so that you and I could be partners, Jaris."

Nicole had trusted her, had thought of Patti as a friend. Turned out she was a monster, a bat-shit-crazy, jealous bitch. She wanted to scream her rage but bit her tongue, knowing the lunatic could snap at any moment. One syllable from Nicole's lips might end this standoff with horrible results.

"You got the drugs from your connection with the Mitrofanovs then?" he asked.

"Yes, I did. The pay is great as are the benefits. Much better than a Chicago patrolman's," Patti continued, the pride in her mania shinning through. "When she tossed her cookies on the commissioner, that was the best day of my life. I took the bag of dope with me to her apartment, ready to end the slut's life. Then you walked in."

"You said it was Nicole's. You even helped me dry her out."

Only Jaris had been my friend back then. Not Patti. Only him.

"I had to. I didn't want to tip my hand. I knew drugging her again wasn't an option anymore for me." Patti's wild eyes sent daggers her way. "I thought I would be satisfied with her being at a desk and me being your partner. I was, for a while. Then you went and signed up with the FBI. I had no clue until Sergei Mitrofanov told me. He was going to put a hit out on you, but I convinced him not to. I had to do a favor for him."

"The missing persons report," Nicole whispered.

"God, you're the stupidest slut on the planet. Shut it. But yes, the missing persons report. I knew you wouldn't question anything Jaris handed you and he trusted me. Just paperwork, which has never been something he took seriously. After Sergei got killed in this dump, I thought my worries were over. Jaris was safe. The report would be buried in the files. No one the wiser. Then your slut here decided to play detective with this small town's sheriff."

Even though Patti seemed to hang on Jaris's every word, seeking his approval in some sick way, he wouldn't be able to keep the madwoman talking forever, despite his best efforts. "So you went to Henry's and found out where Nicole went to."

Nicole prayed Reed and Sawyer would show up. They would come for her. Even though she'd been harsh, they'd made it clear they weren't going to let her go. *Please God, let that be true.* She needed her cowboys right now.

Patti sent Jaris an evil wink. "No. I lured him to my place. I knew Henry would never betray sweet, little Nicole. A dose of Rohypnol in his drink did the trick. He still didn't tell me but I found a text on his cell to Sheriff Wolfe. That was all I needed to put the dots together."

"Where's Henry now?" Jaris asked.

Please let him be alive.

"Still at my apartment. I gave him enough drugs to make sure he didn't wake up. Ever."

"You killed him?" Nicole's head swam with fresh grief. "How could you do that to Henry?"

"Easy." Patti lips twisted into a toothy, horrible smile.

"So you were coming here for the report, right?"

"The report and her. Yes."

"What about the other Mitrofanov man who set the fire? Were you working with him, Patti?"

"You've got it all wrong, Jaris. I called my contact inside the organization. I told the guy about Nicole and what she'd taken to Destiny before I left Chicago. When I got here, I learned the Mitrofanovs had sent a cleanup man to mess with this slut's car. One thing you know about me, Jaris, is I'm loyal. When I found out he'd been shot and was in the local clinic, I wanted to help him escape. Getting past deputy-do-right was easy. A borrowed nurse's outfit and I was in the Mitrofanov's room. When I told him who I was, I knew the truth. He'd been sent not just to get the report back and whatever other evidence Nicole had, he'd been sent to take me out, too."

"You set the fire."

"I did. Lost my favorite lighter, too, in the process."

Patti had been the one to start the fire at the clinic, not the Russian. The man must've been trying to turn off the gas when Doc Ryder and Charlie showed up.

"Jaris, why did you come here for her?" Patti shook her head. "Wasn't I enough for you, lover?"

Lover? "You were involved with her?" Nicole whispered.

"Only a one-night stand after too many drinks," he said softly. "I didn't have a clue she was this gone."

"Speak up or I'll put a bullet between the cunt's eyes right here, right now."

"That would be a mistake, Patti." Jaris put his hands over his head. Nicole did the same. Great police work. The gesture was less about giving in to their attacker and more about letting anyone who happened to look their direction understand what was going down. "The sheriff is in the building behind us. He will be coming out any moment. Do the smart thing and put down your gun."

"Not before I kill this fucking bitch."

This was it. Now or never.

Nicole reached for her gun, knowing she wouldn't have time to get it before Patti pulled the trigger.

Jaris leapt in front of her.

The gun went off.

Nicole watched in horror as Jaris was hit in the head and fell to the ground. Her friend had saved her.

Nicole's fingers touched the butt of her gun but more shots fired.

Patti's lifeless body dropped.

"Chicago, are you all right?" Reed ran up behind her, his gun out.

Beside him was Sawyer, who held his smoking pistol in his hand.

Nicole knelt down over Jaris, feeling Reed's arm around her shoulder. "We need to get the on-call doctor here. He's been shot in the head, but he's still breathing."

She looked down at her *true* friend and then to Reed and Sawyer, the men who had hold of her heart. "Hurry. He saved my life. We've got to help him."

Sawyer nodded and ran back to the courthouse where the temporary clinic had been set up.

Chapter Twenty-One

Nicole hated seeing Jaris in this condition. His head was wrapped in bandages. Only his nose and mouth could be seen. The doctor had just left after delivering the horrific news that his sight might never return. The Denver hospital was sending a helicopter to retrieve Jaris.

"Don't listen to that man, Jaris. He's not even the real doctor here in Destiny. He's just a fill-in. When you get to Denver, you're going to be seen by the best neurologists in this part of the country. They're going to get you back to normal in no time."

Jaris had saved her life, and though he'd not died from Patti's bullet, the price had been high.

"Nicole, I'm glad you're alive."

"Thanks to you," she squeezed his hand.

Jaris was tough. A man's man. He had every right to feel sorry for himself, but he sure wasn't showing it to her.

What kind of life could he have now? Without his eyes, he couldn't be a cop.

"Promise me one thing."

Tears streamed down her cheeks. As much as she wanted to hide her sadness from him, she wished Jaris could see her tears right now. "Anything."

He squeezed her hand back. "Don't throw your life away on regrets. Go after your dreams, Nicky. You deserve happiness."

"So do you."

Chapter Twenty-Two

Reed put his arms around Nicole as she walked out of the judge's chambers, which were currently being used as Jaris Simmons's hospital room. She leaned her head into his chest and sobbed. Sawyer stroked her hair from behind. He and Sawyer owed Simmons a great debt for saving her. He wasn't sure how or when, but he would do his best to repay that debt if it took his entire life.

"He's blind because of me," she cried.

"No, Chicago. He's blind because of Patti. You're alive because Jaris is a hero."

"I can't stand this, guys. It's so hard. He's my friend. He's stuck with me in some of the worst days of my life." Nicole stared at him, her eyes red from crying. "I can't live with this."

"We'll help you, baby," Sawyer said.

"Trust me," Reed kissed her forehead. "I won't leave you to handle this alone, little one. I'm here for you. We both are."

"Jaris just told me to go for my dreams and to stop living a life of regrets. I can't do this if you won't let me in to all of your life, Reed."

"All of my life? You're talking about BDSM, right? Me being a Dom? Your Dom?"

She nodded, chewing on her lower lip, looking so fragile, so feminine it made his heart pound hard in his chest.

"I love you, Nicole. I'll always love you."

"I love you, too, but if I can't be what you need—"

"Let me finish. It's me who was holding back, not you, baby. My brother and you saw it before I was willing to accept it. I was afraid. You're the brave one here. You were ready to dive into my world without any hesitation even though you weren't sure what that meant. Me, I knew, and I still held back. From you. The only person on this earth who can see through my BS, to my truth. The day we talked when Sawyer went to get Chinese food, I knew you were for me—*for me and Sawyer.* You cut through all my crap and I pulled back. I was ready to go vanilla and leave the life I'd known. I'd convinced myself that it was for you I was making that choice, but Sawyer made me see it wasn't for you. It was for me. Selfish me. I'm sorry, Nicole."

"I shouldn't have pushed so hard, Reed."

"Wrong." He cupped her chin. "I fucked up, Chicago. I thought being a Dom was only about control. My control. The only way I knew how to be a Dom was to keep emotions out of the mix. With you, I knew I couldn't do that. I was wrong to hold back. Sawyer already senses there's a sub inside you, and we both know how in tune he can be."

"That's for sure," she said, wiping her eyes.

"You know what I think you need, little one?"

"No. What?"

"A distraction."

* * * *

Nicole walked into the same private room at Phase Four where she'd met Reed and Sawyer. How much had changed since her first day in Destiny?

As Sawyer closed the door and locked it, she felt her heart skip several beats. Reed wore his Dom leathers well. He looked off-the-charts sexy standing by the bench.

"So this is my first day of sub school?" she asked. "We're really doing this?"

Reed smiled wickedly and nodded.

Sawyer came up behind her, also wearing leathers and also hot as hell. "Class is in session, baby. Strip."

"What?"

Sawyer reached around her and pinched her nipples. The tiny sting warmed her insides.

"Starting off on a bad foot, sweetheart. You want to be the teachers' pet, don't you?"

On the way over here, they'd given her a few instructions about protocols. Safe words. How to address them. How they would address her. It all made sense to her in a purely cerebral way. Deeper down, in her core, it was wonderfully terrifying.

"Yes, Sir. I want to be your pet." *Did that just come out of my mouth?* It had, and God it felt so true. She wanted to please them, to show them she could be the woman they needed in every way.

"Good." Sawyer came around in front of her and lowered his mouth over hers. This was a hot kiss, a dominant kiss. Gone was the gentle cowboy he could be. Now, he was all Dom—powerful, demanding, and in charge. Her toes curled as a wave of tingles erupted up and down her body. She kissed him back hungrily, craving more.

"Get her ready, bro," Reed said, his tone so deep and lusty it made her shiver. "I want to see my handprints in pink on that beautiful ass."

Sawyer pulled his manly lips away. "Now don't keep your Masters waiting. Take off your clothes."

Masters? Were they really that to her? They were most definitely masters of her heart, and yes, even her pleasure. The word fit Reed and Sawyer perfectly.

"Yes, Sirs."

"That's a good little submissive." Reed's hungry smile filled her with pride.

Am I really a submissive? Deep down it felt wonderful to turn everything over to them. Every decision, every step, every moment was theirs to guide her through. Even though she was an officer of the law who carried a gun and caught bad guys, with Reed and Sawyer, her Doms, Nicole knew in her very DNA she was a sub.

"Are you going to make us wait?" Reed asked firmly.

She shook her head.

"Our pet is in her head a little too much, I believe." Sawyer, as always, could see into her thoughts with ease. "We'll help you with that," he said, brushing the hair out of her eyes. "I promise."

A wave of dizziness spun in her head as she removed her clothes, leaving only her bra and panties. They'd already seen her naked. So why was she hesitating now? Because this was different. This was a deeper level of intimacy than before when they'd made love to her at the cabin. This was Reed's truth he'd held back and now he was placing it in front of her for her to sample.

"All your clothes," Reed commanded.

"Yes, Sir." Removing her bra first, Nicole felt so small here in this room with them. They'd always seemed tall and powerful to her, but here they appeared to be giants. But they were *her* giants. They'd stolen her heart. Protectors. Lovers. Cowboys. *They're mine, and I'm theirs.* Stepping out of her panties, she felt her heart racing in her chest. She was in the middle of a room at a sex club in a tiny town in Colorado with two hot cowboys—her hot cowboys. What a change her life had taken. She wouldn't go back to the past for all the gold in Fort Knox.

"Time for lesson one, little one," Reed said. Without warning, he and Sawyer lifted her up off the floor and onto the bench facedown. "Spanking 101."

Nicole shivered as anxiety and desire battled within her. To be handled by them this way was something she both wanted and feared.

The first slap of Reed's hand on her ass pulled a little gasp from her throat. More slaps rained down on her ass, some from Reed and some from Sawyer. This was another way they were claiming her. Every time a hand landed on her flesh, a single syllable fell from the lips of her Dom who had delivered the sting. "Mine."

Slap. "Mine," Reed announced boldly.

Slap. "Mine," Sawyer added possessively.

Slap. "Mine." Reed said again.

Slap. "Mine." Sawyer followed.

Over and over. Back and forth.

The thudding was hypnotic to her, blended with their chant. *I'm theirs. I'm theirs.* The symphony of sound and burn took her to a state she'd never felt before. She'd never felt so light, so free. A kind of Nirvana.

Reed bent down and kissed her. "Let's try the paddle on her, bro."

"You think she's ready?" Sawyer asked.

"She's graduated from 101 with flying colors. Time for Intermediate Spanking 202."

A chill went through her. *A paddle?* She was glad Reed was proud of her, but this was supposed to be a toe-in-the-water night, not a drowning by spanking.

Safe word time?

She had her safe word at the tip of her tongue. But even as a sliver of worry shot through her, so did anticipation.

Reed tweaked her right nipple and Sawyer her left. Their fingers tortured her mercilessly. Her clit throbbed and her womb clenched as her want for their touches, their kisses, and yes, even their dominance flooded her entire being.

Was this a kind of recess these Doms were giving her? Just another pop-quiz torment between spankings, the real lesson? Whatever it was, she was getting so very wet with every lick, pinch, and nip from the two Doms.

She'd graduated. Reed had said so himself. How far could she go? She wanted to test her own limits. She trusted her cowboys, her Doms, with her very life. What was a paddling compared to that?

Her whole life she had been forced to be strong and fearless. She didn't regret any of it. The loss. The pain. Even the abandonment by her mother. All of it had made her who she was. But in here, she could let go and embrace her vulnerability. She could let Reed and Sawyer take charge and she could just feel.

BDSM was making sense to her on a level even deeper than she had imagined. More than making sense, she felt herself embracing it, fusing it into that part of her that had always been—her inside submissive.

The paddle came. *Thwack. Thwack. Thwack.* The bite of the thing was like sharp nips. Were they holding back, afraid to go too far with her?

I want to make them proud. I want to be the woman they need me to be. She wasn't sure what the protocol was, but she had to let them know. "I can take more, Sirs."

"Did you hear that, Sawyer?" Reed patted her ass lightly with his hand. "Already trying to top us from the bottom." He laughed.

"I heard her." Sawyer leaned down. "Little one, you've got to be the best sub in this entire club. You're doing great."

"Thank you, Sir." She felt his lips brush against the back of her neck.

"Sawyer, we weren't going to move beyond the paddle tonight with her, but I'm thinking we should keep pushing her. Her responses are honest." Reed kissed her ass. "Fuck, I'm hard as hell. What do you say, bro?"

"Absolutely. Our pet deserves the best night of her life." Sawyer ran his fingers under her, touching her on her pussy, pressing on her clit, making her squirm like mad. "Let's use the mini cat on her."

"Perfect," Reed said with excitement.

"Little one, this is going to sting more than the paddle. Any questions before we begin?"

"What is a mini cat, Sir?" she asked, feeling a new round of trembles roll through her like a shaken beehive.

"Have you heard of a cat of nine tails?"

She nodded. "It's a kind of whip, isn't it?"

"That's right. The one we're going to use on you first has six braided leather tails. Trust me, it's going to take you on a nice ride."

She did trust him. She trusted both of them utterly.

Reed returned with the wicked cat. "You have your safe word ready for us, baby?"

Apparently, her safe word was not only for her but also for them. "Yes, Sir."

"Then let's begin," he said firmly.

The mini cat's first landing on her flesh gave her a hot bite on her ass.

The burn spread out from her behind and through her body, settling deep within her pussy. Sawyer pressed her clit with his fingertips from one hand and pinched her nipples with his other fingers on his other hand. Combined with the leather nips Reed was delivering to her ass, her nipples and clit began to throb in unison, connected by an invisible line.

Even the sound of the cat added to her delicious dizzy state.

Whoosh-crack. Whoosh-crack.

Over and over.

She'd never felt more intoxicated, more alive. Lust swamped every cell in her body. Hunger squeezed at her center. Want surged through every vein, pulsing hot in her blood. Pressure rose inside her to a terrifying level she'd never thought possible. She writhed on the bench, trying to find any sliver of relief, but none came.

Reed and Sawyer are my Masters. No doubt remained inside her.

The cat's strikes ended abruptly, replaced by gentle bites from Reed's and Sawyer's teeth and pinches from their fingers on her naked flesh. They were dining on her like she was their last meal. Being devoured by them sent her even higher and made her even hotter. The crushing need inside her multiplied again and again. Crazed beyond reason, she writhed under their joint assault.

"Our baby shouldn't have pubes." The meaning of Reed's words wasn't hard to miss. "Let's shave her."

"I'll get the warm water and straight-edge razor," Sawyer said eagerly.

"Going to flip you over now, pet." Reed did just that with such ease. She'd never felt so light, so airy before in her whole life.

She looked up into his blue eyes flecked with gold and saw forever there.

"Are you nervous?" he asked as Sawyer came back to the bench loaded with a bucket, towels, and the sharpest, scariest razor she'd ever seen.

She nodded, chewing on her lower lip.

"That's good. From now on, I want your pussy smooth and bare." Reed cradled her chin, making her feel more adored than she had in her life. His eyes held hers completely. "After we shave you, baby, your pussy will be extremely sensitive so whenever we touch you, it will drive you crazy with want."

"Do you trust us?" Sawyer's green eyes had never looked so warm, so possessive, so hungry.

"Yes, Sir. I trust you both," she answered honestly.

"That doesn't mean you aren't supposed to be a little anxious, baby," Reed informed, feathering his lips on her shoulders. "That's all part of this."

Without warning, her mind brought up the image of the moth. It made her giggle "That's good then, because I am anxious but I do trust you, Sirs." From her desk at the station in Chicago, to the guys' back porch of the cabin, to here—about to get her pussy shaved by these two sex-charged Doms—was quite a journey.

Without warning, Sawyer plunged a towel into the bucket. When he pulled it out, she could see the steam rising from the fabric. Surprisingly, he rubbed her underarms with it, warming them up with the water from the cloth. "I'm going to shave you everywhere, little one."

Nicole wasn't about to tell him that she'd just shaved this morning. She didn't think it would matter to him either way.

As he brought the edge of the sharp razor to the softest flesh under her arm, a shiver rolled up her spine. How easy it would be for him to slip and knick her? Easy. She held her breath, listening to the blade scrape against her skin, taking away any random hair it found. The whole thing was exhilarating, turning her into a ball of quivering desire.

With her underarms bare now, Sawyer soaked her arms with the towel, freshly brought up from the bucket of hot water.

"You know why he's doing that?" Reed asked, wrapping his fingers in her hair.

"No, Sir."

"The only hairs we'll allow on you are these beautiful strands." He gave a little tug. "You are mine. You are Sawyer's. Understand?"

"Yes, Sir," Nicole answered, because she did understand from every fiber of her being.

Feeling the blade go up and down her arms gave her several tingles, some hot and others blistering hot. Whatever their temperature, the quakes ended up deep in her womb, causing it to clench hard.

As Sawyer sent the shaving instrument down her abdomen, which she knew had no hair, Reed pressed on her clit, reminding her the final destination for the razor was down there. *On my pussy.*

She moaned, imagining what it would feel like on her most sensitive flesh.

"Now the legs," Sawyer said in a firm tone that screamed in her ears that he was in control. Not her. This was way beyond vulnerable. This was surrender. This was what it really meant to be in a state of complete submission.

"Go ahead, baby. Feel your legs," Reed commanded.

She sent her fingertips to her thighs and was shocked how smooth and silky her skin felt. Sawyer had cleaned her legs better than she'd ever done in the tub with her lady shaver.

Everywhere the blade had been was warm and tingly.

When Sawyer placed a freshly drenched hot towel on her pussy, its liquid mingling with her own juices, she moaned. Over and over, he sent the towel into the water and then placed it on her mound so that even her thighs were soaked.

Reed applied the shaving cream with his fingers to her mound. The pressure inside her was maddening, and she felt her fingers ball into tiny fists and her toes curl into little half moons.

Sawyer held the blade. *A blade? Oh my God!* She was really doing this. This was submission. This was what was meant to be. *They're mine. I'm theirs.*

Her half-hitched breaths came faster and faster, joining the same tempo of her heart, which was beating inside her chest like a racehorse.

She felt the edge of the razor on her most intimate flesh—her pussy. *They're mine. I'm theirs.* Over and over, she silently prayed the words, a mantra that helped her calm her nerves. What she felt between her thighs wasn't a sting or a bite at all. With Sawyer's steady and patient hands and Reed distracting her by pressing here and there on all her erogenous spots—under her arms, behind her knees, along her neck, even under her knees, and more—she was loving every second of her wicked shave. When Sawyer moved back to the bucket to once again soak the towel and clean the blade, Reed would move in and press on her clit, sending her past the brink of deliriousness.

She saw Sawyer wring the cloth out. Still, the steam wafted up from the fabric. Then he gently wiped her pussy with it.

"All done," he announced. "Have you ever seen anything so beautiful in your life, bro?"

"Never." Reed's tone was filled with what sounded to her like awe.

"Really, Sirs?" she asked meekly, bending up slightly to get a peak at herself.

"Let me get the hand mirror," he said. "It'll give you a better view."

Apparently, Phase Four's rooms were equipped with all kinds of things, including *hand mirrors*. She was glad that this certainly wouldn't be her last trip here. What other treasures would she find and experience here? She couldn't wait.

Reed tilted the mirror for her. "See?"

"Yes." Her newly shaved pussy was a pretty shade of pink.

"Fuck, look at our pussy, Sawyer." Reed sat the mirror on the floor, but his wide, unblinking blue gaze never moved from the spot between her legs.

"Damn, I've got to taste our pussy," Sawyer said hungrily.

Why did she love that they called her pussy "*our pussy?*" Another time and another place, she might've thought the caveman-like way he and Sawyer talked about was offensive. But not now. Not here. Not with them.

Sawyer's tongue lapped at her freshly bared pussy, which was even more sensitive than ever before. His tongue and mouth shook her to her core. Every flick of his tongue was even more powerfully devastating than the cat had been, reminding her that he was in control.

As Sawyer licked her into a frenzy of sensations, Reed fondled her breasts, his blue eyes fierce and powerful.

When Sawyer circled her clit with his wicked tongue, she felt her climax approaching. The little flutter deep inside quickly spread through the rest of her body, delivering a much needed release to the immense pressure.

Reed grabbed her wrists. "Ride the wave, baby. That's it. Drown him with your cream."

She could hear Sawyer's licks, and that only multiplied the climatic sensations rolling through her. Her womb clenched and unclenched, again and again.

She moaned so loud that the sound filled the room.

Sawyer's licks became softer, and her arousal began to build up once again.

"Please," she panted. "Please, Sirs."

"Please what, little one?" Sawyer's tone was a mix of wicked delight and primal danger.

"Please. I have to have you inside me, Masters."

"Sweet begging from those pouty lips," Reed said. "Have you ever heard a more beautiful sound, bro?"

"Never."

When she felt them apply lubricant to her anus, she moaned. Never had she felt so hot or gotten so wet before. Her ass was on fire but her lust was even more inflamed.

"She gets an A-plus from me," Reed growled in her ear. His pride made her heart swell and her pussy ache.

"It's unanimous then. Time to give our pet her diploma," Sawyer said.

"Not before we give her our cocks, we don't."

"Agreed."

In the warm hazy state they'd sent her to, she kept her eyes closed as they lifted her up between them. Like before, they sandwiched her between their muscled frames, but this time Sawyer was behind her and Reed was in front. She wrapped her legs around Reed's waist and her arms around his neck.

"We won't always fuck you standing, little one, but it is a position we think you will come to love." Sawyer's words were rich and heavy, sending her into a kind of trance.

"I already love it, Master," she said.

"I can see that in your half-lidded eyes, baby." Reed's blue eyes were bright, holding her enthralled. "This way you must rely on us for everything."

Together, her cowboys filled her up with their cocks—Sawyer's in her ass and Reed's in her pussy. In and out. *Theirs. I'm theirs.* Deeper and deeper. Stretching. Everything inside her rushed to surrender herself to them even more.

Without warning, they both held themselves still, deep in her pussy and ass. Their sudden stillness increased the pressure to a level that was close to terrifying.

"Listen to me, pet." Reed's half-lidded eyes and harsh groan made her shiver. "Destiny is your home. We are your home, your family."

"Yes, Sir. You are." She could feel their long, thick cocks inside her. "I want to please you more than anything in the world."

"Please us? My God, you have in every way imaginable," he said.

"I think our sub deserves her graduation present, Reed," Sawyer said from behind her. "What do you think?"

"I couldn't agree more."

Their thrusts returned, this time more forceful, more demanding.

With their cocks inside her—Reed's in her pussy and Sawyer's in her ass—she felt filled beyond belief. She was between them, burning and writhing.

She felt Sawyer's hand come around and touch her clit, igniting the pressure they'd built up in her into an explosive release. She clawed at Reed's neck and writhed between him and Sawyer as they continued thrusting into her body.

She screamed as the overwhelming sensations created a sea of quakes through her, from her clenching womb and throbbing clit to her tingling skin and electric pulses in her veins. Her body tightened almost painfully and still she came and came and came.

When she felt her cowboys reach their own climaxes, she tightened her insides on their pulsing cocks. She squeezed on their dicks in her pussy and ass. Then two giant, manly sighs, though more like gusts, left their lips. She could feel the heat from their breaths on her skin.

"Baby, I love you so much," Sawyer said softly, kissing the back of her neck.

"I love you, little one." Reed's words were gentler than she'd ever remembered them to be. "With every part of me. Good. Bad. Vanilla. Dom. I love you."

This was BDSM. This was her cowboys' lifestyle. This was her life, now. She deserved this. She deserved them.

I'm theirs and they are mine.

"I love you, Reed. I love you, Sawyer. I love you, Masters."

Chapter Twenty-Three

Sawyer followed Nicole and Reed into Sam O'Leary's lavish office at the tower. Other attendees were already sipping on coffee and eating donuts, though the meeting hadn't started. The group's leader, Sam, hadn't arrived yet.

"Baby, I really don't think you need to be here," his brother said to her as she took a seat in the middle of one of the leather sofas. "Patti was the one who drugged you."

"That's not the point." Nicole smiled and patted the spots beside her, indicating she wanted him and Reed to sit on either side of her. "My support group helped me in my time of need. There are so many great messages you get from these meetings."

Reed shook his head. "You're not an addict, sweetheart."

"Honey, it doesn't matter whether you see me as an addict or not." She kissed him. "I love you."

"I love you, too, sweetheart," Reed said. "I just think you've suffered enough."

"I think you both have," Sawyer said, feeling such joy. "Bro, you've carried so much pain your whole life. You ran from that pain. Nicole taught you to face it. Now that you have, you are living the life Erica and I always wanted for you. Our parents, too, would be so happy you and I found such a wonderful woman."

"You're right about that, Sawyer," Reed said.

"If you'll open your ears, I think what Nicole is trying to say is she is here for many reasons. One of them is to help others." He cupped her chin. "Am I right?"

"I swear you really can read my mind. Yes, you're right." She kissed him. "I love you, cowboy."

"I love you, too."

Sam O'Leary walked in. "Hello everyone. I see some new faces. Let's get started."

Sawyer looked at Reed. "So what do you say?"

His brother smiled and put his arm around their woman. "I say we're all going to be coming to Sam's group from here on."

* * * *

Nicole stood beside one of the four dragon statues in the center of the park in downtown Destiny. She'd learned this one was called the Red Dragon, or as others called her—The Dragon of Passion. The dragon lore that permeated this tiny town was seeping into her heart, not that she would ever admit that to anyone back in Chicago.

She looked over at Sawyer and Reed, who were standing with the rest of the attendees of this ceremony. She'd been with them for over a month now.

Passion.

She'd never imagined how strong it could be, but they'd shown her so much.

She was theirs and they were hers.

How much had changed for her since she'd arrived in Destiny? Everything. The call from Jason had set the ball rolling and now here she was—about to start her new job. But this ceremony was twofold. Looking at Ethel, Gretchen, Erica, and others in attendance—who were wiping the tears from their eyes—reminded Nicole of Charlie, the man who had given his life in the line of duty at the fire.

"Charlie was the kind of man—" Jason cleared his throat, likely trying to compose himself. "He was my friend, my partner." The sheriff looked over at Charlie's former wife and two kids. "Ashley, it means a lot to all of us that you're here. You and your children are important to us, to Destiny. We hope you stay, but whatever you choose to do, we're here for you."

With tears streaming down her eyes, the woman put her arms around her young children. "Thank you, Jason."

"Please join me in a moment of silence for our fallen hero, Charlie Blake."

Nicole didn't know the whole story that had happened between Charlie and his ex, but apparently the citizens here were ready to embrace Ashley.

"Thank you," the sheriff said. "The other reason we have gathered here today is to welcome and deputize our newest member to our town and our county, Nicole Flowers. Officer Flowers is from…"

As Jason continued detailing her law enforcement background, Nicole looked up and saw Henry walking up to join the crowd. Happy tears tickled her eyes. She'd not known he was well enough to come today, but she was so glad he had. According to his doctors, it was a miracle that he'd been able to pull through Patti's drug cocktail. Nicole knew it was part miracle and part Henry's grit and toughness.

Thanks to what she and everyone here in Destiny had done, along with Jaris's testimony, Henry's good name was restored. In a few months, he would be officially retired.

He waved at her from the back. She smiled and waved at him.

Seeing Henry here made her think about her grandfather.

Granddad would've been so proud of her. Though not in his beloved Chicago, she was continuing the family legacy. Since she was little, he'd told her all he wanted was for her to be happy. She looked over at Sawyer and Reed, the two men who she would spend the rest of her life with.

She was happy. So very happy.

"Without further ado," Sheriff Jason Wolfe said, stepping in front of her, holding the badge she would wear. He turned to Ethel O'Leary, the judge of Swanson County, where Destiny resided. The woman stood between her two husbands, Patrick and Sam. "If you please, Your Honor."

She'd been told that the three O'Learys were all in their late seventies. Even so, they were quite the sunny trio.

Ethel grinned. "Raise your right hand, please."

She lifted her hand and felt her own pride swell in her chest.

Judge O'Leary smiled. "Repeat after me."

As Nicole repeated the words, the oath went deep into her being, sealing her to this town, to these people, and to her future.

"I swear that I will support the Constitution of the United States, and that I will be faithful and bear true allegiance to the State of Colorado and support the constitution and laws thereof; and that I will, to the best of my skill and judgment, diligently and faithfully, without partiality or prejudice, execute the office of deputy according to the constitution and laws of this state."

Ethel turned to the crowd. "Allow me to present to you our newest law enforcement officer for our county and our town, Deputy Nicole Flowers."

The crowd applauded.

"Speech. Speech. Speech." Gretchen, Erica, and others in the crowd were chanting in unison.

She hadn't prepared anything. Nervously, she looked over at her new boss, the sheriff. He smiled and nodded. "You'll do great, Nicole."

"Thank you, Sheriff." Then she turned to Ethel. "Thank you, Judge." She looked at the crowd. These were her new neighbors, the citizens she was meant to protect. Glancing at Ashley and her children, she felt for their loss. "I didn't know Charlie well, but I realize I have very big shoes to fill. It's clear to me that everyone in this town loved and respected him. He will be greatly missed." She looked up at her new neighbors and zeroed in on Patrick O'Leary. She'd learned that he'd recently been appointed to the top position of the town after the previous man holding it had been called back to active duty in the Marines. "Mayor, I would like to propose an annual day of remembrance for Charlie."

"That's our girl," Reed said as everyone began cheering.

"That's our deputy," Sheriff Jason added.

"This isn't an official meeting, but it seems the whole town is here." Patrick laughed. "We have a motion. Do I have a second?"

"Second," all of Destiny said in unison.

"So let it be done," Patrick announced.

Ethel leaned closer. "Keep this up, Nicole, and you'll be able to run for mayor someday. I would love for Patrick to step down and take it easy."

"I'm not built for politics, Ethel."

"Either way. Bravo."

After a bit, the crowd quieted.

Nicole smiled. "I promise that I will do my best for the county and for Destiny."

Another round of applause had Reed and Sawyer rushing up to her. They hugged her tightly, each giving her a sweet kiss.

Reed walked to the mike. "Henry Underwood, would you mind coming up her to the podium?"

Nicole wondered what he was doing.

As Henry approached the stage, the crowd stood, also obviously wondering what was going on.

Reed welcomed Henry by shaking his hand. "First, let me tell you how thrilled everyone here, including me and my brother, are to see you so healthy and happy. You're a man of honor and you tried to do your best to keep Nicole safe."

Sawyer moved next to Reed and took the mike. "You're a real hero in our eyes, sir."

The crowd cheered.

Reed turned to face her. "Henry, as you know from our phone call the other day, since Nicole's arrival, Sawyer and I have fallen deeply in love with her."

They called Henry? When? "What's this all about?" she whispered to them, hoping it wouldn't be picked up by the mike.

"Patience, little one," Reed said, and continued. "As we told you on the phone, we feel it is appropriate for us to ask you for her hand in marriage since you are like family to her."

Henry smiled, tears in his eyes. "It would be my honor and pleasure to give my permission to you both. May you always make her happy."

Sawyer and Reed got down on their knees in front of Nicole and the whole town.

"Nicole, you are my world and have helped me see things about myself I never could without you," Reed said. "Would you do me the greatest of honors and become my wife?"

Sawyer took her hand. "Nicole, you are the woman I've always dreamed about, even better than my dreams. You have given us a family again. Would you be my wife?"

Tears of joy streamed from Nicole's eyes. "Yes, yes, yes, to you both."

The crowd roared and cheered.

Reed kissed her and stepped aside. Sawyer was right there to kiss her after.

Erica, followed by Ethel and other locals, ran to them with congratulatory hugs.

Surrounded by so many wonderful people, Nicole glanced up into the clear blue sky for a moment.

I am so very happy, Granddad. I'm finally home.

* * * *

Enjoying the late Saturday afternoon, Nicole sat on the tailgate of her guys' truck with Reed on one side of her and Sawyer on the other.

Every chance she could convince them to take her out to look for Connie, they would. So far, they hadn't seen any signs of the big cat. With Nicole's job as deputy, these outings only occurred a few times a week.

Reed held the binoculars. "There she is." He handed them to Nicole. "Up the mountain, baby."

She peered into the lenses and saw the big cat climbing up to a ridge. "I see her." Connie had fully recovered, getting the vet's seal of approval several weeks ago. Nicole and Erica had cried when they'd taken her to be released, but both of them knew it was what the amazing creature needed.

From the very first, Nicole had felt a connection to the mountain lion. Connie was wild, strong, and self-sufficient.

Suddenly, she saw the big cat stop and turn to her. It seemed like Connie's big golden-brown eyes were focused right on her.

"Can she see me from this far?" she asked them.

"Yes," Sawyer said. "Connie can see much farther than we can."

Nicole gasped when she saw movement in the brush just above where Connie stood. "Oh no." Was the creature strong enough to face another predator? Had they released her too soon?

"There's another mountain lion," she told them.

"It's about time the old girl found herself a boyfriend," Reed said.

"You think it's a male?" She felt him squeeze her hand.

"How's Connie acting around the new cat?"

"She doesn't seem overly concerned."

"Then Reed is right, baby," Sawyer said. "Connie's got herself a sweetheart."

Her heart leapt for joy, watching Connie's new mate brush up tenderly beside her.

I'm glad you got your happy ending, Connie.

Without warning, the two beautiful creatures disappeared from view, heading into the tree line.

She handed the binoculars back to Reed. "Let's call him Charlie."

* * * *

4:59 p.m., Friday—TBK Tower

Reed walked into the TBK building with Nicole and Sawyer. This morning they'd just broken ground on the new house they were building for Nicole—a five bedroom, three and a half bath home not far from the family cabin. It would be a place they could make new memories together with her.

Thirty days. God, had it only been a month since their first night on the back porch with the moth? He smiled, remembering how that little insect had been the thing that had sparked what had become a whirlwind romance. He was in love.

Love? A word he had always found hard to utter. A word he only said to Nicole. It was sacred. Meant only for her.

They were coming to get Erica to take her back up to the cabin. She lived in their parents' old home in town. A change of scenery might do her good. With Eric Knight and the Texans, TBK's new badass programmers, in Dallas trying to weed out the malicious code Kip had planted in their system for a couple of days, Erica's workload was lightened.

Nicole had told Scott about the getaway idea for her, and he had happily cleared the rest of her schedule. Nicole thought Erica could use some girl time to work through the guilt she was still dealing with over the attack in this very building four months ago.

God, he loved Nicole. Always wanting to do her part, to make a difference. Though the town wasn't quite over the loss of Charlie, Reed knew with Nicole as the county's new deputy, the healing would begin.

They came to the elevators that would take them to the top floor where Erica worked as the Knights' personal admin. When the doors opened, out came Jason with Scott Knight and Dylan Strange.

Dylan was yelling into his cell phone, which was quite odd behavior for him. Reed had never seen Dylan shaken like that. Ever. Until now.

Reed's entire body tightened up in instant concern for the only person he believed could have Dylan reacting this way.

"I don't care if he's on vacation," Dylan shouted. "Get on the fucking phone and find Cam now. Tell him to get his ass back here ASAP."

Erica? Something was terribly wrong.

"Flowers, how did you hear already?" Jason asked, his eyes tight with worry.

"Hear what, Sheriff?" Nicole asked.

Dylan turned to her, his ever-present sunglasses not hiding his emotions this time. "Erica has been kidnapped by the Russians."

THE END

WWW.CHLOELANG.COM

ABOUT THE AUTHOR

Chloe Lang began devouring romance novels during summers between college semesters as a respite to the rigors of her studies. Soon, her lifelong addiction was born, and to this day, she typically reads three or four books every week.

For years, the very shy Chloe tried her hand at writing romance stories, but shared them with no one. After many months of prodding by an author friend, Sophie Oak, she finally relented and let Sophie read one. As the prodding turned to gentle shoves, Chloe ultimately did submit something to Siren-BookStrand. The thrill of a life happened for her when she got the word that her book would be published.

For all titles by Chloe Lang, please visit
www.bookstrand.com/chloe-lang

Siren Publishing, Inc.
www.SirenPublishing.com

CPSIA information can be obtained at www.ICGtesting.com
Printed in the USA
LVOW04s0505031214

416755LV00031B/1628/P